JUSTICE FOR ANGIE (POLICE AND FIRE: OPERATION ALPHA)

COUNTERSTRIKE, BOOK 2

CARA CARNES

Cover Design by Freya Barker at RE&D
Content Editor: Heather Long
Copy Editor: Becky Edits

For the latest information, subscribe to my newsletter, or join my Facebook Group.

Dear Readers,

Welcome to the Police and Fire: Operation Alpha Fan-Fiction world!

If you are new to this amazing world, in a nutshell the author wrote a story using one or more of my characters in it. Sometimes that character has a major role in the story, and other times they are only mentioned briefly. This is perfectly legal and allowable because they are going through Aces Press to publish the story.

This book is entirely the work of the author who wrote it. While I might have assisted with brainstorming and other ideas about which of my characters to use, I didn't have any part in the process or writing or editing the story.

I'm proud and excited that so many authors loved my characters enough that they wanted to write them into their own story. Thank you for supporting them, and me!

READ ON!

Xoxo

Susan Stoker

CHAPTER 1

Seven months ago...

"Thanks for picking me up at the police station. That saved a lot of time. Ubers are hard to find in the middle of the night," Angie Bierman commented into the thick silence.

Discussing Uber availability seemed safer than the fact that she'd spent too much of her life in the Philadelphia police station the past several weeks. At least the latest attack hadn't ended with a trip to the hospital. The knife wound along her back from the attack two days ago ached at the thought.

"You didn't call me," Claude clipped, his voice more angry than hurt. "You should've called me after you phoned the police. After you were attacked, not hours later when the police were done questioning you."

Angie tensed. The man she'd hired as her assistant manager had a valid point. Then again, he also had more than friendship in mind. She'd avoided the awkward conversation so far, but the latest situation hadn't helped.

"I'm sorry. Things happened faster than I expected. By the time I realized I'd forgotten to call, I was already at the police station. I didn't expect it to take so long. The last time didn't."

Nor had the time before that.

"Three attacks in less than two weeks likely has them worried. Finally. Are they going to do anything about this shit?"

"They'll try to have a cruiser patrol around the dojo more often around closing," Angie said.

"You're kidding me. That's all?" The man's anger thundered through the vehicle. "Tell me you're done poking your nose into this."

If he knew exactly how far she'd "poked," he'd be pissed. She hadn't told him or anyone else what she'd done. She was close, though. Why else would she be getting attacked so often?

Noah Wints had to be guilty.

The attacks and the threats and phone calls had to mean something. She was close.

"They arrested the wrong man. Hannah's ex didn't do it."

"That's not our problem."

But it was. If Detective Shuler was too stubborn and lazy to look into the murder properly, then Angie would. The young woman who'd been murdered had been a member of Angie's dojo since it opened.

Angie shoved thoughts of the woman's murder aside as Claude pulled into a parking spot outside Angie's place. Cool air brushed across her when she exited the vehicle.

"Are you sure you don't need to go to the hospital?"

"No, I'm fine." Aside from bruised ribs, the worst injury was a punch to her eye. An ice pack and a couple Tylenol, and she'd be fine. She turned and headed toward her apartment. "Thanks for the ride."

"Don't you dare walk away from me, Angie. We aren't done discussing this." Claude shouted the last words.

Angie forced a deep breath. Darkness enveloped the small parking lot, but she charged onward. Heavy footsteps fell behind her. Damn it.

"Claude. Stop." She spun and faced down the irate man. "I'm done with this discussion."

"Like hell you are! I'm not going to stand back and watch you get yourself killed." He grabbed for her arm, but she punched his stomach and glared. Hands up at his sides, he took a step back. "Okay, sorry. You have to listen to me. I can help keep you safe, but you have to back off."

"I'm not backing off. Someone murdered Hannah. She told me herself she thought she was being followed. The police have been screwing around with her investigation for weeks now. She deserves justice."

"They've arrested her ex."

"Eric couldn't hurt a kitten, much less a strong woman who had decent defense skills. She wasn't afraid of him. It was someone else." Angie fumbled with her keys as she arrived at her door.

"What do you mean by someone else? What did she say?"

"Just that a car was following her. She got a partial plate. I have a DMV list April got me." She'd had the list for quite a while, but he didn't need to know that.

"God dammit, Angie. This is the shit I'm talking about.

You can't go off like fucking Nancy Drew. Someone killed Hannah. Now Chastity's in the hospital."

Angie's eyes burned. Chastity had been brutally attacked—beaten and raped. The young woman's words still haunted Angie two days later.

They did this because of you. They said it was a message. Back off or the next one dies. This is your fault. I'll never forgive you. Get out! Get out! Get out!

Angie breathed through the emotional tidal wave drowning her insides. "I don't want to talk about her, Claude."

"Christ, you're still blaming yourself, aren't you?"

"You heard what she said. She was a message delivered for me."

"Then why the fuck are you still looking into Hannah's murder? You've been attacked three times. You should buy a fucking clue and back off."

"And what? Watch Hannah's murderer get by with what he did? Watch whoever attacked Chastity get by with it?" Angie opened her apartment door and flicked on the living room light. She tossed her purse on the sofa and kicked off her shoes.

"I'll handle Chastity's shit. I can keep you safe, Angie, but you've got to let me do that." The man followed her into her apartment. "Destroy that fucking list April gave you and let the police do their job. They'll find Hannah's murderer."

Right. The detective in charge of the investigation had a suspect in custody. Why look anywhere beyond Hannah's ex? Eric was the perfect patsy so the Philadelphia Police Department could declare another case closed. Easy peasy.

She'd already poured through the DMV list, comparing registered owners of black SUVs to dojo members and clients. She'd found a match—a very recent one.

Noah Wints, a local, rich playboy, had hired Angie for personal lessons less than a week after Hannah's murder. Coincidence? Possibly.

"You aren't saying anything," Claude accused.

Angie kept quiet because the overprotective man following her as she entered her kitchen would blow a gasket if he knew she was already neck deep in an investigation of Noah Wints. She'd broken into his home office and rifled through receipts and paperwork. He'd been to the club Hannah stripped at several times.

He'd known her.

A few receipts wouldn't be enough evidence for a lazy detective, though. Angie needed more, which was why she'd decided to escalate her efforts. More personal classes at Noah's mansion. Sooner or later, she'd get the evidence she needed to nail his ass.

Assuming he didn't have her arrested. Wints had caught her snooping more than once. So far, he found her "nosiness" amusing. But now the threats included phone calls she hadn't told Claude about. And the attacks were worse than before.

That had to mean something. Right?

One way or another, Hannah's murderer would pay.

So would Chastity's attacker.

"Angie, talk to me. I can't keep you safe if you don't

trust me." He touched her shoulder as she grabbed a water from the fridge.

She was close and the threats were intensifying, which meant she didn't need Claude or anyone else trying to help. The only people who could—the cops—weren't interested in listening. So, until she got enough evidence to prove Noah Wints killed Hannah, she was on her own.

Angie turned and regarded the man who'd become her closest friend. "You're a great guy, Claude. One hell of an assistant manager. And a friend. I need you to trust that I know what I'm doing and stay out of this."

"Stay out of what? You're up to something. You've been gone from the dojo more and more. Those threats are getting worse."

Angie's gaze flicked to the stack of threats, photocopies of the originals she'd given the police. Most had arrived via the dojo's printer. Someone had hacked the dojo's WiFi network and sent threats. That alone would terrify anyone.

But Angie didn't back down when scared. She'd been raised by a career military officer, one who'd taught her and her sisters to face an adversary and stand their ground. You didn't run from an asshole threatening you.

You kicked their ass and taught them a lesson.

She'd been proficient in four martial arts before she was a teenager, a black belt in three. She'd added a black belt in Krav Maga and extended her skillset since graduating high school. Whoever had chosen to make her a target when she'd started investigating Hannah's murder had underestimated her.

Then they'd learned a lesson and started going after people near her.

Chastity.

"I'm going to go see Chastity again. Last time didn't go very well, but I want to see her before she's discharged—which will be tomorrow," Angie commented into the tense silence. "You wanna go along?"

The man's jaw twitch. Fire illuminated his brown eyes. "I want to know what the hell you are up to, Angie. Let me protect you."

"I can protect myself."

"The last attack was two people. Whoever is doing this is escalating. You need help."

The last attack before tonight had been the only one, so far, to end with a hospital trip because someone had stabbed her in the back. Although the wound hadn't been deep, it'd required a few stitches.

"The police department is aware of the attacks. They don't have the manpower to provide protection, nor do they believe they're related to Hannah's murder."

"Are they blind?" Claude motioned toward the stack on her coffee table. "They have the threats, right?"

"Yes, but they're vague. They're warning me off, but they don't say off what. The police aren't convinced it's related. I haven't exactly been a welcomed presence in this neighborhood." Angie shrugged. She'd pissed off more than a few of the local thugs by teaching the local kids how to defend themselves. Even adults were taking her self-defense courses now.

"Bullshit!"

Angie took another sip of her water and glared at her

hot-headed assistant manager. They'd become closer friends the past several months, but she'd recently noticed his interest in her went much further than hers in him—which was why she'd started distancing herself from him. She couldn't risk alienating someone so integral to her business by rejecting his personal advances.

"Claude, you know I don't like your temper," Angie whispered. "I know you're frustrated. So am I."

He ran his hand through his hair and sighed. "Sorry, I just don't want you hurt by this asshole. I care about you, Angie. Lots of people do."

"If things get any worse, I'll take a few days off and hole up somewhere. I'll go visit my sister in California, or my dad." She sat on her sofa and waited until Claude sank into the chair across from her.

"I could go with you."

That wouldn't happen, but Angie didn't reply. She'd been raised by the stubbornest human born, so she knew when to not argue. If the time came to lie low, she'd vanish. Then she'd let Claude know. He'd run the dojo in her absence.

Everything would be fine.

But she had zero intention to run.

* * *

Six and a half months ago...

Angie pressed herself into the darkened corner of the abandoned warehouse and willed her breathing under control. One labored breath at the wrong moment and she could end up dead.

"Angie..." The masculine sing-songy voice dragged her name out as boots scraped against the concrete floor. "Come out, come out, wherever you are."

Angie snagged her cell phone and dialed 911. Her labored breaths sawed in and out as she waited for the call to connect. Police wouldn't arrive in time, but she needed to call. Cover her ass for what was about to happen.

"9-1-1."

"I'm at the abandoned warehouse on Chester and Main. Three armed men are trying to kill me. Please send police." She ended the call without waiting for the woman to ask questions.

"You've been a very bad girl, Angie. Tell you what. You come out now, and I'll let you pick how you die. I'll make it quick like Hannah got, or I'll give it to you long and rough like that other bitch got it. But you won't be breathing when I'm done with you." Delight resonated in the man's voice. "Fan out. Find her. She's here somewhere."

Adrenaline flared within her as she shoved out of her hiding spot and navigated her way through the maze of debris strewn about the warehouse floor. Dust stirred with each cautious step. Pale moonlight beamed in via broken windows along two walls.

She ignored the chatty leader holding a Sig Sauer and focused on the man nearest her. While she held her own against anyone in hand-to-hand and street fighting style combat, guns and knives proved more of a challenge.

A lead pipe about the length of her forearm drew her attention. She squatted and grabbed the potential weapon, tested its weight. It'd do. Her first target kept his gun at his side rather than aimed in the direction of his gaze.

Idiot.

She waited until he walked to the other side of a half wall. The moment he turned his attention from where she skulked in the shadows, she struck. Two direct strikes to his knees. One, hard, bone-shattering crunch of pipe to his forearm. She punched the gun from his hand with a quick strike to his wrist.

Pained screams sounded from him. She kicked him beneath his chin, leaned downward as his weight crashed to the ground. Angie snagged the weapon and returned to the shadowed corner.

And waited.

Her pulse pounded its fury. She focused her attention on the sounds. Footsteps crunched glass.

"Fuck! Wood? Boss, Wood's down!" The agitated voice rose. "She fucked him up bad."

"Shut the hell up, you idiot." The second man's voice had lost the sing-song tone of delight from earlier. "She couldn't have gotten far. Check upstairs. I'll go the other way."

"Right."

"Fuck the orders. We're killing this bitch quick."

The freaked-out asshole headed up the stairs, which creaked with his weight. The boss's voice boomed a few seconds later.

"Yeah, it's me. The bitch took Wood out. Get the others into position. We'll take that fucking bastard Claude out first. Then we'll see if she's ready to play nice. The kids'll be next."

Fear clawed Angie's insides. No. No. No.

Claude would handle himself, but the kids? The only kids she knew were the local ones who took self-defense classes at her dojo. The man's voice shouted the orders. No, they weren't orders. They were a trap—one to force a knee-jerk emotional reaction rather than a strategic defensive one.

Angie forced the fear aside, locked it away and waited until footsteps sounded and gave the bastard's location away. She maneuvered into position and dealt two strikes to the back of his knees. Her weight fell atop him, her knees in the center of his back. She whipped his head back, then slammed it face-first into the concrete.

The gun rattled from his grip. She grabbed it. She flipped him over and gripped his throat as he blinked to awareness. The gun pressed against his temple.

"Who hired you?" Angie demanded, her voice low with rage. "Tell me who the fuck hired you, and I'll let you live."

"Fuck you! You're a dead bitch walking."

"Tell me." She slammed a knee into his groin and relished the cries of pain. She grabbed his cell phone and shoved it into her back pocket. Her grip on his throat tightened until the bastard's eyes widened. He clutched her hands with his, but there was no escape. "I'm low on patience for this bullshit. Who hired you?"

"Don't know," he wheezed. "Just hired to fuck you up, warn you off."

"Yeah, well I have a warning for you. Back the fuck off everyone you were told to hit to get to me. You even think of touching them and I'll fucking gut you." She pulled the man's phone out, punched the last number and held it to his ear. "Now's when you show if you're smart."

Angie pushed the speaker on and squeezed the man's throat tighter until he nodded his assent.

"Yeah."

"Stand down." The man wheezed the order. "We ain't getting paid enough to fuck with this crazy bitch."

"Boss?"

"Stand the fuck down."

Angie clicked the call off and tossed the man's phone aside. Sirens sounded, their proximity close. Although she'd remained on scene for the previous attacks, this one was different. Whoever was after her had ordered them to go after the kids in the neighborhood.

Angie couldn't let that happen, which meant it was time to run. Lie low. Wait.

Footsteps sounded from the creaky stairs. Opting to ignore the third thug rather than get caught by the police, Angie fled the warehouse. Her breathing was labored by the time she'd run back to where it'd all started—outside her dojo.

"Angie?"

She whirled toward the voice. Benny and his brother, Clay, approached. Both teenagers had wide eyes. They held spray paint cans as they always did. "Tagging tonight?"

"Maybe." Benny shuffled forward. "Been looking for you."

"Oh yeah?" Angie approached the kid, locked gazes. "You found me."

"Shit went down after you left the dojo earlier. Cops

showed up with a warrant." The kid looked her up and down. "You've pissed off someone really connected."

Angie fisted her hands and looked around. Three days ago, police had pulled her in as a potential suspect for an attack on Noah Wints. While she wanted nothing more than to wail on the asshole, she hadn't done a damn thing to the bastard.

"You know what they were looking for?"

"I know they didn't find it 'cause the kid hired to plant that shit's got a big mouth. Clay and I got wind of some shit being planted at the dojo for the cops to find and take you down. We found it. Flushed it." Benny glared at his brother. "You had Clay's back when he was gonna do stupid shit. Now we've got yours."

Shit. Angie couldn't risk going back to the dojo now. She'd intended to warn Claude about the threat against him and the kids before she got out of town to lie low for a while. But the cops could still be watching her business, waiting for her to return.

"Word on the street was there was a hit on you. You okay?" Benny's gaze slid over her once again. For a seventeen-year-old, he saw more than most likely did. His hands fisted.

"Yeah. They're handled, but you need to get the word out that whoever's doing this shit might be coming after you and the other kids from the dojo. The cops will be around. I need you to give them that info, Benny."

"We don't narc to cops."

"This ain't narcing. This is being smart," Angie said. "You give them that info, Benny. It's up to you two to keep everyone in your hood safe. Don't let me down."

"Why can't you tell them?" Clay asked.

"I'm going to ground a bit until the heat blows over."

"That's smart," Benny said. "Glad you aren't too proud to lay low when necessary. You need a place, I know some boys on the other side of Philly."

"I'm good. This conversation didn't ever happen. You got me?"

"Yeah. I got you. Like I said, you did Clay a solid and kept him out of trouble. We've got your back." Benny glanced around. "I'll get the word out and I'll tell the cops. Not that they'll give a shit."

She'd kept Clay from joining the local gang a few months earlier while Benny had been in juvie. The younger boy had been susceptible to their influence without his big brother around to keep him safe. Angie had been nearby when they'd cornered him in an alley, and she'd intervened. Benny and Clay had been hang-arounds at the dojo ever since.

"Tell Claude, too."

"Yeah. Whatever."

"You tell him I'm hiring you to do a mural on the dojo. Whatever you want." Angie waited when the two brothers looked at each other, eyes wide.

"For real?" Clay asked.

"For real. Get that done. Lose the tagging. That's beneath you both. You're wicked talented. Give that to my dojo, then maybe others will let you do their joints."

"Cool." Benny nodded. "We've got your back. For a white bitch, you're pretty cool."

Whatever. Angie got into her car and drove away. She'd kept a go bag in her car with clothes, toiletries, all the cash she'd hoarded at her apartment. There'd be no reason to go back there until this mess was over.

Someone was hunting her.

Until she figured out who and somehow stopped them, she couldn't return. Too many lives were at risk if she did.

CHAPTER 2

Present day

Chicago

Angie Bierman woke. Pulse pounding, she vaulted off the dingy motel bed. Hands fisted and body in fighter stance. Her gaze swept the small room. What had roused her from the restless slumber exhaustion finally demanded?

Sirens blared in the distance, a common enough sound in the rough neighborhood that served as her latest hiding hole. Chicago was the tenth city in six months. She'd hoped it'd last longer than a few days.

The empty beer can alarm she'd made out of trash remnants and string jiggled as the door handle moved. Wood shattered into the room as a mammoth-sized man with a jagged, green vine tattoo along his neck entered. A second aimed a gun at her as his goatee-clad face erupted into a grin. Malevolence darkened the third man's dark gaze as he entered the fray.

Angie raised her hands in mock surrender and waited.

Her heart thudded hard in her chest as adrenaline surged. "You don't want to do this."

"Shut up." The second man flicked the safety off on his Sig Sauer. "You're coming with us."

"I'm afraid that won't happen." Angie waited until the three men entered the strike zone. "This is your last warning. Tell me who hired you, then leave."

The first man chuckled and adjusted his belt. "She's a cocky bitch."

"She won't be when we're done with her," the second commented.

"That's not the job," the third said as he looked at the first man and pulled out a cell phone. "Tie her up, Tiny. I'll make the call. Easiest five grand we've ever made."

So much for handling this the easy way. Angie took a step backward and to the left when Tiny approached. The move kept the gun toting asshole in strike range. She surged upward, struck Tiny's knee, then the gun-clad man's wrist with a two-strike hit of her feet.

Tiny cried out as he tumbled to the ground, but she was already kicking the side of his head and slamming her head into the second man's face. Blood sprayed across her. The hot splatter barely registered as she grabbed the man's face and slammed a knee where her head had hit.

The third man's eyes widened. He reached for a weapon, but Angie kicked his legs from under him and kneed his nuts while slamming her elbow into his throat. Tiny crawled toward her, his meaty arm reaching for his waist.

Idiot.

She slammed a fist into the third man's face then

vaulted upward as Tiny shot. Pain lanced her side, but the momentum surged her forward and into the startled man. Her legs wrapped around his neck as they landed on the ground. She forced her body left. The distinctive snap bolstered her with more adrenaline as the man fell limp to the carpet.

The second man remained unconscious, a fact Angie's mind processed a second before returning to the third bastard with the cell phone. She grabbed the device, shoved it into her pocket, then grabbed the man's throat.

"Who hired you?" Angie gritted out the inquiry even though she knew the idiots didn't know.

None of the others had a clue who had hired them. Local idiots never second-guessed an "easy payday." Blood seeped from the bastard's nose and mouth. He grasped his throat, but didn't speak.

She punched his groin, waited as he cried out in pain. Voices sounded from the hallway. Damn. Witnesses were the last thing she needed right now.

"Who. Hired. You." She enunciated each worth as she grabbed the man's shirt and loomed in his vision. "I can snap your neck like I did Tiny's, or leave you bleeding here with your other man. Your choice."

"I dunno." The man wheezed the words. "Just a guy on the phone. That's all I know."

Another dead end.

Angie stood, grabbed the backpack from the side of the bed, and yanked out the small digital camera she'd stolen in Cincinnati. She snapped pictures of the three men and left the room. She needed someone to substantiate what she already knew—Noah Wints was trying to kill her.

The slippery bastard left no evidence trail, though. All Angie had were suspicions and a mountain of circumstantial bullshit the authorities had refused to accept. Until they did, she was on her own. On the run.

"Call the cops," an older black woman shouted from the doorway of a motel room down the left of the hall.

Angie headed right, past two scrawny men with bloodshot eyes. Her left side burned. Blood coated her hand when she touched the area. Damn. Tiny's shot had hit. Pain coursed through her when she ran down the stairs.

Get away.

Hide out.

Assess the injury.

She locked her mind down. She'd process what she'd done later—if she survived the latest murder attempt. Cool air struck her when she exited the small motel. Sirens sounded from ahead of her, so she went right, down a block and then angled into the alleyway she'd marked as exit pattern two.

Buses ran every fifteen minutes. Luck was on her side when she arrived at the stop and climbed on behind two black women in platform shoes, short skirts and barely-there tops. Both turned, eyes wide when Angie stumbled into a seat.

"You need an ambulance," one of them said. The bus lurched forward as it continued down its route.

Angie twisted until she sat semi-upright, her hand pressed hard on the injury. She grabbed the second woman's wrist when she pulled out a phone. "No. No cops. No ambulance. I'm fine."

"You're bleeding." The first woman snapped her gum and shuffled past Angie to sit on her left. "Lemme see."

The woman's touch was gentle as she dragged Angie's hand away from the injury. Her curly, dark hair tumbled down and obstructed her face a moment. Wide, dark eyes peered up at Angie as some of the color leeched out of her beautiful dusky skin. "You've been shot."

"Shit." The second woman reached over from the seat to Angie's right. "You in trouble?"

"You could say that." Angie sniped the reply and blinked until her vision refocused.

"I'm Vani," the woman on her right said. "My friend there is Isa. We'll get you sorted."

Great. The last thing Angie needed was well-meaning innocents tangling themselves up in her mess. She fought back the refusal lodged in her throat. Arguing with the two of them would only draw more attention from the few folks on the bus.

Isa rested a hand on Angie's upper back and guided her forward. She lifted Angie's blood-soaked shirt. "I think it's a through-and-through."

Vani tapped on her phone. "We know a guy, a nurse. He helps us ladies out when we get into trouble and don't want attention, if you know what I mean."

Angie gritted her teeth and grimaced through the pain as the bus made another stop. A couple people stepped on, shuffled past. One paused, looked down.

"What the hell are you looking at?" Isa snapped. "Move on. Mind your own damn business."

"Whatever. Bitch." The man spat angrily as he continued on.

"No cops," Angie repeated.

"Slow your roll. We've got you," Vani said. She reached over and yanked on the overhead cord. "Isa's man lives around the corner. Ben can meet us there."

Vani put a jacket around Angie's shoulders as the two women steered her off the bus and down a darkened sidewalk. Angie darted her gaze around the area. People milled about stoops leading into tall buildings she assumed were apartments.

"What the fuck?" A man rose from his perch atop a step. Anger harshened his voice. A couple other men hovered near him. "Isa?"

"What the fuck you waiting for?" Isa shouted. "Get the door!"

"Bitch, you ain't bringing your mess to me." The man opened the door and glowered. "Shit, she's bleeding."

"No shit, Einstein," Vani said. "You dumbasses gonna help, or stand there watching?"

"Fuck." Isa's man surged forward, lifted Angie up.

Blackness assailed.

* * *

"SHE NEEDS A HOSPITAL."

Angie blinked awake and surged upward, but a young man smiled and gently pushed her back. "You're safe. Settle back before you rip the stitches out."

Stitches. Angie leaned back on the dark blue sofa and glanced about a small living room. A lean black man stood nearby, his arm draped around Isa. Vani sat on a coffee table beside a man in green scrubs. He had green hair and the kindest eyes she'd seen in a long time.

"I'm Ben. What's your name?"

"Angie." She looked at the two women. "Thank you."

"Girl, you've lost your damn mind," Isa said. "You need a hospital."

"No." Angie shook her head. "I've gotta go."

"You aren't going anywhere right now," Ben said. "Are you in trouble?"

"I'm fine," she lied.

"Fine doesn't get me called to stitch up a gunshot wound in the middle of the night." The man snipped off a piece of tape with a small pair of scissors and settled it against Angie's skin. "We got the bleeding stopped. Got you cleaned up."

"Thank you."

"You need this checked out. There might be internal damage I didn't see."

"I'll be fine."

"I know people who will help if you're in trouble. Isa and Vani think you are." Ben put the scissors in a small bag near Vani. "Police were called to a motel near the bus stop you got on at."

Damn.

"Word on the street is Tiny's dead," Isa's boyfriend said. "Fucker deserves it, but word'll spread fast that you're here. Lynch and his crew have eyes everywhere. She can't stay here for long. I don't need that trouble at my door. My kid's asleep in the next room."

Ben's gaze narrowed. "Angie, you're going to have to

trust me when I say I know people who will help. Whatever trouble you're in, they can get you sorted."

"I can't drag anyone into this," Angie argued. "You've done enough."

Lynch. She had another name. She filed the information away and willed herself to get off the sofa. Get out of the apartment before anyone found her. The forty bucks she had left wouldn't get her far, but she'd figure something out.

She always did.

Ben pulled out a cell phone. "I'm going to make a call, put it on speaker. Listen to what he says, then we'll figure out the next step. Okay? I've helped a lot of people in trouble thanks to this crew I'm gonna call. They can help."

Angie wished it was that simple. Rather than argue, she leaned her head back on the pillow and willed the pain away. Ben took her hand and squeezed as the line rang.

"This is Jade."

"Hey, man. I've got someone here who needs help. Angie's been shot. Looks like there was an altercation of some sort here. A local thug was killed." Ben paused. "She has evidence of recent injuries."

"Angie?" The man's voice boomed through the cell phone. "I'm Jade. I facilitate entry into a network to help people in trouble. The more information you give me, the safer I can make you."

Angie swallowed. Remained silent.

"Who's after you?" Jade asked.

When she made no reply, Ben squeezed her hand.

"This network has never failed anyone they've helped, Angie."

"Someone's hunting me," Angie admitted. "I can't prove who, but he hires local thugs to capture me wherever I go. Ten cities now. Six months. I'm sorry. You can't help me with this."

Silence descended a few heartbeats. Jade sighed heavily. "The shit you call in isn't ever easy, Ben."

The man smirked. "You wouldn't want the simple problems."

"True that." Jade paused. "Zero D's restructured the network. I'm gonna route the call to Counterstrike. They're an organization that's helping run things now. If things are bigger than they can handle, Zero tags in her crew. I'll be honest. There ain't much Counterstrike can't handle."

"Thanks, man," Ben said. The line went quiet several moments.

Unease pricked Angie's skin the longer she waited. Every wasted minute increased the risk someone would find her. Exhaustion demanded she give Ben's contacts the chance to help. Running had gotten her nowhere.

"Angie? My name is Twitch. I'm going to help you get to a secure location." The man's gravelly voice boomed from the speaker. "Ben, I understand she's not alone with you."

"No. There are three others here. Several more saw her enter this apartment," Ben said. "She was shot, too injured to move."

"She's stable now?"

"As stable as I can get her," Ben said.

"Okay, good. Can we trust those around to keep quiet about this?" Twitch asked.

"What the fuck?" Isa's boyfriend shouted. "I ain't no snitch."

"I'm more worried about you talking if whoever is after her puts pressure on you," the man said. "I determine how best to contain the situation."

"She killed someone in a local thug's crew," Ben said. "At least, that's what we're assuming based on police activity near where she was."

"Angie?" Twitch asked.

"I had no choice. They attacked." She swallowed the revulsion rolling through her. It'd become too commonplace to justify the blood on her hands, the damage she'd done to stay alive. "This wasn't the first attack, won't be the last."

"It will if I have anything to say about it," Twitch replied. "Ben, someone will be in contact in a few hours. They'll want the names of everyone there now and as much information as possible on the altercation."

"Understood."

"Angie, are you strong enough to leave on your own, or do I need to send someone to retrieve you?" Concern softened the man's words. "I need an honest answer."

"I'll manage." Angie sat up. Dizziness overcame her a moment. She eyed her backpack in the corner of the room, near the door.

"She's lost a lot of blood," Ben said.

"I'll manage," she repeated, her voice stronger than before.

"Very well. We'll trust her judgment for now, but you

can take her the first few steps until she's out of Chicago, if you're okay with the risk. You understand what that means."

"I do." The man's lips thinned. "I'll get her out safe."

"Get her out of there. Take us off speaker. I'll give you instructions once that's done."

Angie stood, leaned against Ben. "I can't let him endanger himself any more than he has. I'll do it alone."

"Let him help you, girl," Vani pleaded as she stood.

"Thank you for saving me." Angie hugged the woman. Then repeated the action with Isa. "I can't risk any of you more than I have. I wish I could repay your kindness. Please, let me do this alone. You've done enough."

Silence ticked by a few more moments. Twitch sighed heavily into the phone. "Fine. I'm going to trust that you can do this alone. But the first sign of trouble, and I'm sending someone to help you."

"Fair enough." Angie gritted her teeth and ignored the achy throb along her injured side.

"Call me if she gets into trouble," Ben said.

"I will." Confidence exuded from Twitch. Angie clicked the speaker off when she took the phone.

Determination kept her standing. She looked down, noted someone had changed her shirt. She picked up her backpack and winced as pain lanced her side. The corridor outside the apartment was empty. Thankful for the lack of witnesses, she exited the building.

"I'm out. What now?" Angie said.

"Now we get you safe. The network uses relay stations and inventory caches. That means you'll have a series of stops before you get to your final destination. Each one will resupply you with what you need, give you a chance to rest up and eat. It'll also give me a chance to make sure you aren't being followed."

"How? How can you make sure I'm not followed?"

"I can watch surveillance cameras in the area and see if the same people are at more than one stop."

Wow. Her pulse quickened. "Twitch, I'm not sure this is safe for you. Or whoever this network is."

"Let me worry about that, Angie. The nearest cache is five blocks south of your current location. I need you to be honest. Are you able to walk that distance, or should I send someone to pick you up? It'll take a while for me to secure someone."

"I can walk." She didn't want anyone else involved. She'd endangered too many people. "Twitch, I'm worried about Ben and Isa and Vani. Isa's man has a kid."

"I'll make sure they're safe."

Angie wasn't sure why, but she believed him. Maybe the exhaustion weakened her doubt. She headed south. "Where am I going?"

"There's a parking garage on the corner of Brackshire and Garfield. Are you familiar with the area?"

"Not exactly." Angie huffed a laugh. "I've only been here two days."

"Sounds like you've had a rough go."

"That's an understatement."

Angie remained quiet, forced one foot in front of the other. Unease crawled along her skin as she plodded down the sidewalk. Exposed.

Weakened.

She was a bit surprised the man on the other end of

the phone hadn't drilled her with ten thousand questions. The silence, however, was a welcomed respite. The lack of conversation kept what little energy she'd bolstered laser-focused on getting to the parking structure on Brackshire and Garfield.

"I'm almost there." She panted the statement into the phone when she saw the structure.

"Good. I know this will be hard, but I need you to trust me. There's a black Honda Civic in Slot 122 of the garage. Keys will be on top of the left driver's side tire."

"Okay." Angie continued forward.

"You need to disconnect this call and toss the phone as far away as you can, after you remove the SIM card."

"But—"

"This is where you trust me if you want to stay alive." The man's voice brooked no argument.

Angie debated whether she should trust the stranger, who'd gotten her to a parking garage where a car supposedly awaited. Ben had patched her up and sworn the network would help her. Counterstrike. Twitch.

Everything sounded…

Military.

"You're former military. That's where the name's from," she guessed.

"That matters to you?"

"Yeah. My father…" She paused. Then forced another deep breath despite the pain along her side. "He's INSCOM."

If the guy was former military, he'd understand what that meant—U.S. Army Intelligence and Security

Command. It was a test, one met with silence for longer than Angie expected.

"You need that test taken, Angie, I'll give it to you. Then you trust me to get you safe." The man paused. "I started off Army, spent most of my time within JSOC."

"Task Force Green," she whispered the guess—one met with silence. She wouldn't expect anything less from a former Delta Force operative. Her father always said you could tell more about a man in what he didn't say. A man who'd served his country honorably didn't boast about what he'd done.

"I'll toss it." She swallowed. "Thank you. I have phones from the men that attacked me."

"Toss them, too. We'll get everything we need from them without risking those phones being tracked." Twitch paused. "Once inside the car, there'll be another phone in the glove compartment. Turn it on. Answer when it rings."

"Okay." She clicked off, yanked out the SIM card, then tossed the cell phone she'd been using and the extras she'd grabbed from the attackers onto the ground. She crushed them beneath her right heel, then proceeded to the parking garage across the street.

CHAPTER 3

John "Twitch" Stanz expended a relieved breath when the call ended. His boss, Milo Davenport, remained silent as he loomed behind him. Middle-of-the-night phone calls for the network weren't ever good because they meant someone was in desperate need of help.

Counterstrike was one hell of an organization, one Twitch had joined up with the moment he'd left the service. Milo, along with his twin brother Ethan, had founded the organization to help domestic violence victims and others needing help.

The network was the latest initiative toward that endeavor, one started and run by The Arsenal, the best private paramilitary organization around. One heavily tied to Counterstrike because one of the six Mason brothers who ran it had saved Ethan's life.

"Status?" Milo asked.

"She's on route to the car," Twitch said. He activated The Arsenal's HERA system and called up the surveillance cameras within the area. One nearest the garage captured

Angie's face. The security system sent data from the real-time facial recognition scan. "Son of a bitch."

Angie Bierman. Arrest warrants and BOLOs from Chicago, Atlanta, Cincinnati, and a string of other locations rolled across the screen, but the first dataset was the one that drew his attention. The start of the woman's nightmare.

Philadelphia.

She'd been flagged as a person of interest on the murder of a local woman, Hannah Plast. He typed in the victim's name into HERA, along with Angie's and hoped the system they'd recently been trained on using would pull up more information.

"We may need to run this by Zoey before we insert her into the network," Milo commented. "You mentioned JSOC. Why?"

Zoey, aka Zero D, had designed the network before she'd started working for The Arsenal. She was brilliant and fiercely protective of everyone protected within it. If anyone potentially going into it was higher risk than "normal," Counterstrike needed her approval to proceed.

Twitch thought it was sad that people needing help had to be categorized into threat levels, but Counterstrike had already seen why several times. The network was no longer as underground as it'd once been, which meant it was at risk from crazies either wanting to find someone in it or destroy it entirely.

"She needed a pulse on whether she could trust me. Her father's INSCOM." Twitch keyed in the woman's name and entered the government databases. He'd know who the man was soon enough.

The genius women who helped run The Arsenal had designed one of the best damn offensive and defensive security systems around. HERA ran interactively with every database the elite organization had access to. It also hacked into security feeds and operated just about anything the user was smart enough to use.

"There's a string of assaults and dead bodies in this woman's wake," Milo said. "We need her isolated until we figure out her story."

Twitch understood his boss' hesitation. Too many innocent people relied on the anonymity and safety The Arsenal's underground network provided. It was up to Twitch, Milo, and the rest of Counterstrike's operatives to vet anyone before their pasts got erased and they were given a new start on life.

After Counterstrike, and The Arsenal if needed, made their trouble go away.

Twitch waited longer than he wanted to call the second phone number listed within the cache's inventory. Thousands of asset caches were strewn about the country for people to use if needed. Vehicles, medical supplies, clothes, cash. Weapons. The list of supplies and services trusted volunteers within the network provided was endless.

"Did Ben burn himself with this?" Milo asked.

Ben was one of Zoey's most trusted assets within Chicago. Even though Counterstrike had only helped a few clients in the region, most of them had gone through Ben. His file within the network's database was extensive.

An incoming chat within HERA opened. Twitch read the message. Zoey was online and in the network, running the situation. "Doubtful. Zoey's sending Medina with a team. They'll contain the Chicago situation and let us know the fallout." That left Twitch's sole focus on Angie—a fact he was grateful for.

"Twitch?" Angie's voice broke at the end. Heavy breaths tumbled through the speaker. "I have the car on."

"Good. There should be a small, black zip pouch inside the front console. It'll have enough cash to get you to the next safe zone." Twitch paused. "Are you okay? Do you need medical attention?"

"I'm fine." The woman gasped. "There's a lot of money here."

"Hopefully you won't need it all, but we'll be ready for whatever comes. Okay?"

"Where am I going?"

Great question. Twitch had personally only cycled two people through to Counterstrike's Austin headquarters since they'd taken the task on. Patch handled most of them. Ethan's cell phone rang.

"Yeah, Zoey." Milo's voice stilled Twitch's movement. If the woman was calling, it was likely The Arsenal was fielding what happened next. All the outstanding warrants and police interest in Angie stirred enough trouble to necessitate caution. "Right. We got it. San Antonio."

Okay. San Antonio. The declaration didn't surprise Twitch. Counterstrike and The Arsenal had more than a few friends in assorted law enforcement branches in the city an hour away from both Counterstrike and The Arsenal.

"You're going to Chicago Executive Airport. It's about

twenty-three miles northwest of your current location," Twitch said. "Turn on the car's GPS and I'll give you the address."

"It's a destination on the stored locations," Angie said. "I—I have warrants. I think. Is an airport safe?"

"This one will be. You won't be alone, okay? We'll have eyes on you when you arrive at the airport."

"Right. The surveillance cameras."

"Fly her into Austin. Zoey wants an extra waypoint before San Antonio," Milo ordered.

Twitch switched the private jet's destination. Dread settled in his gut as more information about Angie Bierman's past six months streamed across the screen. Who the hell was this woman, and who was after her?

"This is your client," Milo said.

Ethan typically ran point on protective details, but Milo had recently taken on the task more to free his brother up to spend time with his new fiancée, Marisol. The couple had been through a lot the past several months, but Twitch had no doubt they'd handle anything that came their way. No one at Counterstrike would let anyone harm the beautiful woman who'd won Ethan's heart.

Twitch grunted. He rarely took the protective detail on the people they helped because his size tended to intimidate or outright scare most of the abused women and children Counterstrike typically helped. At six foot five and two hundred sixty pounds of solid muscle, Twitch towered over most everyone.

But Counterstrike was low on operatives and had more open cases than they could manage as it was. Milo and Ethan never turned anyone down, though—especially someone within the network.

"Understood."

A last-minute case meant coordinating his personal life. Counterstrike took priority for almost everything except his mom. Someone would need to help her out. Twitch pulled out his cell and typed out a message to his sister. His sister, Bea, didn't spend time with their mom unless she was told to—a fact that had worried Twitch on more than one occasion.

The cell rang moments later. Bea.

"Hey, sis."

"Don't 'hey sis' me. What do you mean I need to spend time with Mom? I go on Fridays."

"I've got a case."

"So?"

"So she needs someone checking in on her," Twitch said.

"Bullshit. She's fine. You're a worrier. I'll text her a couple times a day like I always do. She'll phone if she needs anything," Bea argued.

"Sis, she's not doing good," he said.

"She's got the wheelchair, and it's only another couple of weeks before the knee replacement surgery. John, you need to stop ordering me around. I've got enough shit to deal with. I can't do your shit, too."

His shit, too.

Their mom wasn't shit. She was a strong and fiercely independent woman who refused to ask for help even though she needed it, which was why he made it a point to check on her regularly. She had two bum knees, which had caused her to fall on more than one occasion the past couple of months.

But his brain honed in on the heart of the trouble. "What shit do you have to deal with? You've gotten wrapped up around another asshole. What was his name? Mike. Is he causing trouble?"

"That's not your business," she snapped.

"Seeing how my crew and I always have to handle the assholes when things go south, it is my business." He glanced at Milo, who was frowning, and made a mental note to check into Mike.

"Whatever. I'm too busy to babysit Mom. She'll be fine."

"Check on her," he growled.

"Fine!" Bea hung up.

"Everything okay?" Milo asked.

No. He couldn't assume Bea's stubbornness would go away, which meant their mom wouldn't have anyone checking in on her while Twitch was protecting Angie. He shoved the phone back into his pocket. "I might need a couple of check-ins with my mom while I'm out. Bea's being difficult."

The man's jaw jerked a few times, but he nodded. "We'll make sure to check on her. And Ryan."

Ryan, Bea's son, remained a focal point within Counterstrike's daily operations. Twitch, Ethan, Milo, and several other operatives made it a point to check in on the seven-year-old.

One of these days, his little sister would grow up and start making better decisions. Until she did, it was Twitch's job to see to her and his nephew.

"Twitch?"

"I'm here, Angie. I'll be here with you until we get your troubles sorted. How are you doing?"

"I think someone's following me. I made an extra few turns before getting on the highway. A red car's made all of the same turns. I'm not sure I can fight them off easily." The admission was coated with fear. For the first time, Twitch sensed the woman's fear more than her anger and exhaustion.

"She's hurt worse than she admitted," Milo commented. The man sat beside Twitch.

"You aren't alone. We're going to get you through this," Twitch said. He called up a map of the area, then correlated it with network assets.

Fortunately, Chicago was a large hub within the underground network, which meant there were more volunteers present than many other locations. Although there were multiple ways to shake someone following Angie, Twitch wanted eyes on her. He needed an independent assessment of her condition.

"There's a twenty-four-hour diner on the corner of Wilks and Elk. Park on the street and go in. Take the cell phone and the money. Leave the keys in the car." Twitch hoped there was parking nearby. He couldn't have her exposed for long, especially if someone was following her. "Don't leave the car until I tell you. Okay?"

"Okay."

Twitch opened a second phone line and called the asset at the diner. If he wasn't working…

"This is Matt."

"Matt, this is Twitch from Counterstrike. I've got someone outside the diner needing help."

"You're lucky I'm here," the man said.

"You send your schedule in. Our system keeps it with your contact number." Twitch clicked the money sign by the man's name to send payment for his help. "She's got a tail and is wounded. I need her secured."

"On it. Send her inside. I'll get her tail handled."

Twitch clicked off with Matt. "Angie, there's a tall man named Matt who's going to help you. He has spiked blond hair and is working inside the restaurant. Make your way inside and he'll help you."

"Okay."

* * *

ANGIE KEPT THE PHONE PRESSED TO HER EAR AS SHE GOT out of the vehicle. A tall man with spiked blond hair stood just outside the restaurant's entryway. Her pulse pounded quickly as she headed toward him. The red car pulled into the parking lot, but no one got out.

No one attacked.

Witnesses.

Adrenaline streamed through her as Matt moved toward the red car. Cell pressed to his ear, his voice boomed through the parking lot. "Hey, man. It's Matt over at the diner. I've got a red car that just pulled up. They're following a woman who's scared out of her mind. Can you swing by and get them locked down?"

Matt rattled off a license plate a few seconds later as he clasped her upper arm. "Thanks, man."

"Who was that?" Fear harshened her tone.

"My brother. He's a cop."

Angie tightened. The red car took off.

"You're safe," Matt said.

"No cops," she whispered.

"He won't be trouble. Come on, I have half-hour left on my shift, then I'll get you secured." He scanned her. "You need to eat and get something to drink. You look like you're about to pass out."

"I-I can't just go in and eat."

"Yes, you can." Twitch's calm voice on the other end of the line dragged Angie's attention from the fear crawling through her insides. "Go in and sit down. Eat. Matt and his brother will keep you safe until we figure out if anyone else is going to show up and try to hurt you."

"They left. I should go before they get back."

"You aren't going anywhere alone right now, Angie. You need to trust me. Go inside, sit down, and wait until Matt says it's safe to leave."

Angie squeezed her eyes shut. "Okay."

She clicked off the call and followed Matt inside the restaurant. He escorted her to the booth at the back, farthest from the door.

"Are you a vegan, vegetarian, or one of those who won't eat carbs?"

"No." She slid into the booth and grimaced as pain rushed through her side. "I'll eat whatever's quick."

Matt returned moments later and set a huge sandwich with fries in front of her. A glass of water and a soda appeared next. Angie glanced up at the man and froze when she saw a cop saunter up beside him. Both had the same pale blue eyes and light blond hair.

The cop sat in the booth across from her. Matt glanced between both, but left without comment.

Damn. Damn. Damn.

She focused on slathering her fries with enough ketchup and pepper to drown their existence in a red and black swirl of yumminess. Her stomach growled as her trembling hands unraveled the silverware from the napkin. Unease clenched her stomach muscles, but she forced her gaze to the man studying her as though she were a bug.

"Hi, I'm Angie. A friend of Matt's." She picked off the tomatoes from the sandwich.

"I'd almost believe that if you weren't picking off tomatoes from a sandwich he brought. He's obsessive about details and wouldn't ever forget how a friend took their food," the man commented with a grin. "Eat, Angie. I'm off-duty whenever he calls. Even if I wasn't, I wouldn't do anything to put you in more danger than you're in."

She picked up the sandwich, took a big bite before her shaking hand dropped it. Chewing kept her from saying something she shouldn't. Was the cop part of the network? She wished Twitch was still on the phone.

Matt returned and set a burger and fries in front of his brother, along with a soda. "Let her eat in peace."

"I am." The man glanced up at his brother. "Is this another one I pretend I never met?"

"Yep."

"Then you should probably get her some different clothes. Dried blood can only get ignored so long." The man picked up his burger and took a bite. Chewed. His gaze slid to the plate in front of him as if he hadn't just informed her she had dried blood on her.

She glanced down, noted the substance near her elbows and up the back of her arm.

Damn.

She continued eating. There wasn't much she could do about the dried blood. Truth told, it didn't even faze her, not like it should. She'd done far, far worse than leave assholes bleeding in a dingy motel.

Matt returned, dropped a long-sleeved button-down shirt on the booth beside her. "Put that on."

"Thanks." She donned the shirt, gaze locked on the cop, whose jaw twitched.

"One of these days, you and I are having a long conversation about all these 'friends' you keep putting me in front of," the man commented.

"That conversation's not happening tonight," Matt said. "I'm off in twenty. We'll need a ride."

"Of course you will." The man sighed when he was left alone with her once again. He glanced at her from across the booth. "Eat. You're safe."

Right. Safe with an off-duty Chicago cop less than two miles from where she'd left three assailants—at least one of which died. Her stomach soured with the thought, but hunger and determination won the internal struggle. She'd process what she did later, when she was secure.

Would that ever happen?

She inhaled the sugary soda along with her food. She stared at the empty plate and willed away the hunger still agitating her stomach. There'd be more food later. The money Twitch had given her would see to that.

The cop pushed his soda and untouched fries toward her, along with the ketchup and pepper. She smiled her gratitude. The cell phone rang a few seconds later.

"Hello?" She eyed the man across from her warily.

"I'm sorry, Angie. I know you're scared, but Matt's brother is safe. He's not part of the network, but he's helped us out a few times. I didn't know he'd be called, but he'll keep you safe." Twitch's voice settled her.

"Okay."

"Matt said you almost swallowed your food whole. It's been a while since you've eaten." Concern deepened his voice.

"I guess so." She couldn't say much more, not while a cop hung on every word she offered. "Matt's almost off work."

"I know. We can keep this line open while they take you to the airport, if you want."

"Yes. Please." She hated how much trust a stranger had already earned. Twitch had kept her safe so far. "Thank you."

"Set it down and finish eating," Twitch said. "I'll stay on the line until you're in the air."

Angie set the phone down and picked up the ketchup. She slathered a layer on, then doused the fries with pepper. The cop chuckled and leaned back into the booth.

By the time Matt was off work, her stomach was stuffed and her nerves were semi-calmed. She carried the cell phone in her left hand as they exited the restaurant. Unease pricked her skin when she saw the squad car.

Matt's brother opened the back door. Smiled. "You ever been in one of these?"

"Shut it," Matt growled. He climbed into the back and motioned toward Angie. "Come on, get in. He'll drop it off and get his truck a few blocks from here."

Right. At the police station where his fellow cops were likely typing up a BOLO for her. Fun times. She remained silent and climbed into the back. Hopefully this would be the one and only time she was in the back seat of a police cruiser.

"Are you going to stay on that call the whole way?" The cop glanced in the rearview mirror.

Angie brought the phone to her ear. "Probably."

Twitch chuckled in her ear. The sound kept her focused on something other than the car pulling into the parking lot of a police station. It stopped several feet short of a gated entry. The driver threw it into park and got out. Opened the back door.

She followed Matt out and stood beside him as the cop and his car disappeared through the gate. "This has got to be the weirdest thing I've done."

"Oh, I'm betting that's not true," Twitch teased.

Angie smiled. The action startled her. Then she realized what the man on the other end of the line was doing. "You're good at this."

"At what?"

"Keeping me distracted enough to not be scared."

"You're doing great, Angie—way better than most people would. Hang in there a bit longer."

Matt's brother pulled up in a black dual-cab truck. She

climbed into the back while Matt took the front seat. The vehicle pulled out.

"Where are we going?" his brother asked.

"Chicago Executive." Matt's response was curt, offered no room for discussion or argument.

She caught his brother's gaze in the rearview mirror. "Thank you."

"Don't thank me. I was never here. I never saw you."

Right.

Angie settled back and willed the dull throb where her bullet wound was away. For now, she was safe, thanks to a stranger named Twitch, Matt, and his unnamed brother who was a cop. And a nurse named Ben. And two women who'd helped her not bleed out on a bus.

The list of people who'd helped her in Chicago was long, but those who'd been hurt because of her was also lengthy. Did Tiny have a family? She squeezed her eyes shut and forced the guilt aside. He'd chosen to take the job —one which would've ended in her death if she hadn't defended herself.

The excuse was wearing thinner every time she used it. Sooner or later, her luck would run out.

She just hoped that when it did, no one else died because of her.

"Make a circle before we drop her off," Matt ordered. "Someone followed her to the restaurant. I wanna make sure we're alone."

"You think I can't spot a tail?"

"I think she's in more trouble than most I've helped. Circle a couple of times before we drop her off." Matt glanced at her from the front seat. "Are you going to be okay going the rest of the way alone?"

"I'm not alone." She pointed toward the phone she had pressed against her ear.

"Right. Tell him this one's on the house. No way in hell I'm getting rewarded for helping an injured woman being chased by assholes that was so hungry she inhaled her food."

A gasp escaped Angie at the man's angered words. "He—"

"I heard him, Angie. He's already been paid."

The network paid people to help? How the heck did they get the money to do that? Questions rolled through her mind, but she kept quiet. Now wasn't the time to open that can of worms.

The man's brother caught her gaze in the mirror again. "I'm thinking it's time I have a conversation with whoever's on that phone, brother. If that's the sort of shit you're doing, I'd like to help. Officially."

The truck circled the small airport a couple of times before it stopped at the farthest hangar. Angie climbed out of the backseat and looked at Matt, who'd rolled the window down.

"Thank you."

"Good luck." He looked over at his brother. "Head out."

"I'm not leaving until she's in the air."

Right. Angie headed toward the hangar. She'd gone four steps when Twitch's voice sounded in her ear.

"There's a small Cessna just outside the hangar. A man with gray hair will be there. He's flying you to Austin, where I'll meet you."

"Okay." Angie continued until she spotted a wiry man with gray hair.

The man didn't offer any conversation as he opened up the plane and motioned her inside. She went in and took a seat. Buckled in. Head leaned back against a leather seat, she expended a relieved breath. Was this really happening?

"Get some rest, Angie. I'll see you soon."

"Thank you, Twitch."

CHAPTER 4

Confusion clouded Angie's mind for a moment when she woke. An older man stood a couple feet away, his face grim with worry as his gaze narrowed. "We've arrived, ma'am."

Right. Austin.

Relief overrode the worry she'd carried the past several months. For once she wasn't alone with the nightmare. No matter what happened next, she wasn't in Chicago. She had cash in her pocket, which meant she could run if needed.

Always have backup plans.

She deplaned and turned the cell phone on. It rang moments later. "Twitch?"

Darkness blanketed the quiet airport except for floodlights spotlighting the tarmac. The small plane had landed away from the primary area commercial flights used. She turned a full circle and froze when she noted the black Escalade parked nearby. Two tall, muscular men stood near it.

One of them waved. "You're almost to us, Angie. I'm waving."

Angie's pulse quickened. She ended the call and shoved the cell into her pocket. Pain shot along her side, but she lumbered forward. Twitch was far taller and bigger than she expected—a veritable wall of muscle at least six foot five. The man beside him was only a few inches shorter. Both had dark hair. Strength and confidence exuded from them. But her focus remained on Twitch, the man who'd stayed on the line while she ate her fries across from a cop because he'd sensed she was terrified.

Thick, black hair long enough to run her fingers through accentuated the rugged handsomeness of his jawline and obsidian eyes. The latter drew her in, as if offering a peek into his soul. A dark green T-shirt stretched across his wide shoulders and broad chest. Thick, corded arms adorned with tattoos above the elbow drew her attention. Her gaze traveled downward to lean hips and thick, powerful thighs.

Twitch took a step forward and held out his hand. "Hi, Angie. I'm Twitch."

"Hi." What now? Her heart thundered in her chest as her gaze swept to the second man. Both were muscular, carried themselves like former military. Taking them both down would be...

Difficult.

"This is one of my bosses, Milo Davenport. He and his brother Ethan own Counterstrike." Twitch touched her upper arm. Warmth seeped into her skin from the contact. She visually scanned the area once again.

Milo's lips thinned as he followed her gaze. "We're going to help you figure this out, Angie."

"Come on. Let's get you somewhere safe." Twitch motioned toward the vehicle.

Angie sat in the backseat and kept her backpack in her lap as the two men got into the front. Milo guided the vehicle out of the airport without comment, but his gaze met hers in the rearview mirror several times. The silence gave her time to get her mind calmed.

They'd need information.

Answers.

She only hoped they'd still help her once they heard about the things she'd done the past few months. Guilt and dread settled in her stomach, a lead weight she didn't want. It'd been so long since anyone believed her.

"Twitch mentioned your father is INSCOM." Milo met her gaze in the mirror once again. "I never had the pleasure to work with him, but several people I admire have spoken highly of him."

Angie tightened. "He's not involved with this." None of her family was. The less they knew, the safer they'd be.

Not that her father or Mia needed to be protected. They'd handle any trouble without problem. Rose was another story. Her younger sister lived life in the naive, geeky sector. The biggest worry she had was whether the code for her latest creation worked.

"Counterstrike works with another organization, The Arsenal. Have you heard of them before?"

Angie nodded. "Twitch and Ben mentioned them."

"Right." The man's voice softened. "We're concerned

with what we've discovered so far, Angie. Whoever's hunting you finds you too easily."

No shit. Angie bit back the fear lodged her throat. "Does that mean I'm on my own now?"

"No," Twitch said. "It means we've got a few extra steps to go through before we can get you situated somewhere. You aren't alone. We're going to help you with whatever this is."

Relief stilled Angie's thoughts. She hugged the backpack. One thousand, seven hundred and fifty dollars. She'd counted the cash from the Honda three times. That'd keep her running for a while if things went sideways.

The vehicle parked in front of a small shop on a darkened street near downtown. Unease kept her quiet as Milo shut off the vehicle. Assess the situation, then react. She exited when the two men did.

Twitch put a hand on her back as she read the sign outside the building. Hank's. A bearded man stepped from the shadows.

Milo met him halfway. "Thanks for coming out, man."

"Anytime." The man's gaze swept across Angie. He motioned toward the building. "We aren't open until noon today. Lock up after you're done. Leave the keys in the pot."

Then he left.

Angie watched the stranger get into an SUV and leave. What the hell?

"Come on." Twitch guided her toward the door that Milo had already opened.

The small eatery was exactly what one would expect.

A long L-shaped bar ran along one wall. Assorted tables took up most of the space, except for a small dancing area toward the back. She followed the two men through the dining area and to the back. Past a kitchen. Into an office.

Milo opened a door and entered another room.

"We have a safe room here we sometimes have to use," Twitch explained.

Angie swallowed. Dread settled within her as she walked through the small area.

Twitch's obsidian gaze remained on her. He traced his fingers along her cheek. "It looks like you have a few more injuries we didn't know about."

Angie hadn't registered the abrasions and bruises from the Chicago attack. The bullet wound had negated all other pains. "They'll heal."

"I'm thinking you've dealt with too many injuries the past few months," Milo said.

Angie didn't comment. What could she say? She looked about the small room. A set of lockers hugged the wall along the right side. A bathroom took up the area beyond that. Benches sat in the front of the room. Weapons and ammunition filled the left wall.

Angie walked to the weapons wall and ran her hands along the knives. A small assortment of nunchaku filled the bottom portion of the wall. Her hands itched to grasp the black nunchucks, test their weight. It'd been too long since she had a pair.

"You know martial arts," Twitch said.

"I owned a dojo." She paused. "I still do, I guess."

"What disciplines?" Milo asked.

"Karate." She always started with what everyone

expected. It was easier to not admit to the others, but both these men were former military. They likely expected more. They'd know it took more than basic karate to survive what she had. "Jiu Jitsu. Mixed Martial Arts. Krav Maga. I've studied quite a few others."

"That's an impressively eclectic assortment," Twitch said.

"It's benefited me." She forced her attention from the array of weapons. "What now?"

"Now you shower and change into clothes you'll find in the bathroom. The duffel bag beneath the sink will have clothes in assorted sizes. Use whatever fits best. We'll get you more clothes later." Milo crossed his arms. "Leave everything on you in the trash bag beneath the sink. Toothbrushes, paste, brushes, and anything else you'll need is in there."

Right. Someone named Zoey wanted her scrubbed. Angie hadn't realized that meant literally. She nodded, too grateful for the help to argue. Matt's brother would be glad to know the dried blood would be gone soon. Truth told, nothing sounded better than a scalding hot shower and fresh clothes. Except for maybe a real bed.

She headed toward the bathroom, but Twitch halted her progression with a hand about her waist. "You'll need to leave the backpack, Angie. We have to inspect everything you keep with you from this point forward."

"I need everything in here." She glanced down at the pack. "It's important."

"Then it'll come with us. While you're showering, we'll make sure there's nothing else in there. Whoever's chasing you is finding you too easily."

"You think he's tracking me?" Angie shook her head. "I've been careful. No phones. Nothing with GPS. Ever."

"It's just a precaution," Milo assured her. "We'll be waiting here until The Arsenal's doctor comes. They're choppering him in from their compound. We want to make sure your injuries were properly tended."

"I'm okay."

"We'll make sure you are," Twitch said. "Go and shower. Change. Take your time."

* * *

TWITCH PACED THE AREA RIGHT OUTSIDE THE SAFE ROOM and waited. The Arsenal had choppered their doctor and a team to Austin. Logan had been with Angie for more than half an hour now. What was taking so long?

"You good?" Milo asked.

No. Someone was hunting a woman down as though she was an animal. How the hell does that happen?

Medina and his team were outside. "I thought they were going to Chicago."

Milo folded his arms in front of him. "She sent a different team to Chicago. Medina is Angie's protective detail. They'll assist however you need."

"Is San Antonio still the play?"

"Yes. Cruz will take a formal statement from her."

"The FBI has jurisdiction?" Cruz Livingston was one hell of an agent, one who had helped them on multiple occasions.

"Her situation is somewhat unique. Depending on what we find out, the FBI could investigate her being stalked across state lines. Either way, Jennifer is her legal counsel. We'll get the charges we can dropped."

Jennifer Davenport was a bulldog of an attorney. Twitch was grateful the woman would help Angie. "Fuck, man. I'm not sure how she's lasted this long."

Angie was beautiful. Long, silky black hair that tumbled down her back in a riotous mess she hadn't seemed bothered by. Long, muscular legs meant to wrap around a man, not…

Damn.

Twitch ran a hand down his face and silently admitted what he couldn't voice. He was attracted to the woman. Milo would drop him from the protective detail if he knew, which was why Twitch kept quiet.

He wanted to see Angie out of this mess.

"She's an impressive woman," Milo said. "Zoey suggested a different play."

"Which is?"

"Put her in a safe house. Situate her in a new life. See what happens." Milo's eyebrows rose.

"Use her as bait?" Twitch thundered the inquiry. "She needs protection."

"She'll have that. Drones are in the safe house. An Arsenal team and you on her six."

"We don't even know who's after her yet." Twitch paced once more. The move was smart, but not safe for Angie. Hiding her until they got some answers made more sense.

"Which is why I told Zoey that wasn't an option. Yet. If this situation doesn't get resolved easily, we can revisit it and ask Angie what she wants. She doesn't strike me as a woman who'd hide if she can stand her ground."

Twitch knew better than argue. Milo was right, and Angie deserved a quick resolution. If the idiot came after her with Twitch and an Arsenal team protecting her, then he'd get caught. No one would touch her.

The door opened.

Logan exited first. Angie followed. She rubbed her arms.

The sweatpants she wore sagged around her smaller frame. Although she was at least five foot five, Twitch felt like a giant. Hell, he was compared to just about any woman he'd met.

Four martial arts.

Angie could handle him and anyone else.

"Is she clear medically?" Milo asked.

"Ben did a great job. I'll leave some pain medicine in case she needs it. She likely has a few bruised ribs from a previous altercation. Keep the wound clean, but she should be back to normal in a couple of days at most." Logan smiled at Angie. "She's tougher than most people I know."

"What's next?" Angie yawned the question. Red tinged her cheeks. "Sorry. I suddenly got really tired."

"That's expected. You've run on adrenaline a long time." Logan looked at Twitch. "Get her secure. Let her rest. Everything else will wait."

"That's the plan." Twitch settled a protective arm at her back. "Come on. Let's get you to the safe house."

* * *

ANGIE LEANED FORWARD AND PEERED INTO THE SIDE mirror. "Someone's following us."

"That's Medina and his team. They're from The Arsenal. They're going to help keep you safe."

There was an entire team? "That's a lot of people. I have money I can get to in the morning."

"We aren't taking your money," Twitch said. "Have you been in contact with anyone since you left Philadelphia?"

"I sent a few emails from libraries and other WiFi spots, mostly to my dad. I was afraid he'd mount a nationwide hunt for me otherwise."

"He likely would have. Does he know anything about this?"

"No."

"Who else did you contact?"

"Claude. He's my assistant at the dojo. I told him I needed some time away."

"Six months is a long time away. When was the last time you contacted him?" Twitch looked over.

"Three months ago. He wasn't happy. He'd sent quite a few emails last time I checked. So far, things have gone okay without me."

"That was three months ago."

She clutched her stomach and let the worry chew her insides as the vehicle headed down the freeway. Claude had done a great job keeping the dojo operational from what little she'd found via Internet searches. She'd watched the website and noticed the class schedules being added. "He said we'd lost about a third of our members."

"They'll come back once you're home. It must've been

hard to walk away from a business you worked so hard to get open."

"How did you know I worked hard?" Suspicion raised her voice.

"I'm just guessing, Angie. Any business takes a lot of hard work to get started. A cousin of mine opened a Mexican restaurant in Austin. I saw what he and his family went through getting it running. It took a year before they were operating in the black."

"It took me about that long," she admitted.

"I'd imagine you had a bigger challenge. Stereotypes run rampant in some industries."

Angie looked down at her hands. "No one wanted to learn martial arts from a white woman. What the hell did I know? They wanted someone like you."

Twitch chuckled. "I'm thinking word got around fast enough that you knew what you were talking about."

"Eventually. Once I became more active in the community and started holding free self-defense courses, people showed up for private lessons. The mostly-empty classes filled up."

"How many people do you have working for you?" Twitch asked.

"I hired Claude seven months after I opened the dojo. He was one of my first members and had an extensive background. He'd recently moved to Philadelphia." She looked over and noted the man's firm jaw. "You think someone I work with is involved."

"I suspect everyone until they're proven innocent. You should, too."

"That's why I haven't contacted anyone."

"You've been very smart from what I've seen, which makes me wonder how he's found you so easily. We didn't find anything in your stuff." Twitch looked over. "What about outside of work? Friends? Boyfriends?"

"Pfft. The dojo opened at six every morning and stayed open until ten at night. That was my life," she admitted. "I don't make friends easily and dating was…"

Angie wasn't sure how to admit the problem she had with relationships without sounding conceited. Men were either intimidated by her martial arts skills or too weak to impress her. She wasn't attracted to a man unless he could handle himself against her.

"I'd imagine a lot of men won't date a woman who can kick their ass," Twitch said with a chuckle.

"Or they tried to prove they could beat me." She looked out the window. "Dating became a contest."

"That's crazy."

"Not all men are like you, Twitch. They aren't walking brick walls."

He laughed. "Well, for what it's worth, I don't exactly have a line of women knocking my door down."

"Why the hell not?" Heat crept up her cheeks. "Never mind. Not my business."

"I'm intimidating to most women. They assume I'm a muscle-bound meathead. When they find out I was in the service, it gets worse. Or they hear about my work at Counterstrike and… it's an issue."

"It shouldn't be," Angie whispered. "What you and your group does is important."

"So is what you do. I saw your website. Most of your work was geared toward women and children."

"Martial arts techniques can be modified to be more effective for people my size or smaller. Learning them from someone the same size can help." She smiled. "I took the presumed disadvantage and marketed it as a strength."

"That's smart," Milo commented.

The quiet man hadn't spoken much, but she'd noted his gaze on her often. He was definitely former military, likely spec ops from what she'd observed in the way he maintained a vigilant assessment of their surroundings.

"I found a niche."

"So no pissed off exes?" Twitch asked.

"I'll give you a list so you can run them, but none are a threat." Angie hoped Twitch and Counterstrike found something she'd overlooked. The sooner the nightmare was over, the better.

CHAPTER 5

Voices woke Angie. It took a moment for her to remember where she was.

A safe house in San Antonio.

With Twitch.

She rose from the bed more rested than she'd been in a long time. The wound on her side was better than she expected.

She wandered out of the bedroom and down the hall. The three-bedroom, two-bath home in a central San Antonio residential neighborhood was far nicer than she'd expected. Shock registered when she entered the living room.

Four men sat with Twitch.

She remembered Medina, but the other two were strangers. Unease pricked her skin when she saw the badge one of them wore on his belt.

"Angie." Twitch stood. "I'd like you to meet Cruz and Quint. Cruz Livingston is with the FBI. Quint Axton is with the San Antonio Police Department. Come and sit."

"W-why are they here?" Angie hated the fear in her voice.

Both the strangers looked at one another. Grim expressions filled their handsome faces.

"We aren't here to arrest you," one of them said. He stood and offered his hand. "I'm Cruz. I've worked with Counterstrike on quite a few cases. I hope we can help with yours."

She noted the kindness in his eyes and hesitant smile. Quint rose and shook her hand as well. Both men sat after she and Twitch did. The latter took her hand.

"We need to get a statement from you," Medina said. "The more we find out now, the easier it'll be to get some answers."

Angie nodded and motioned toward her backpack. Medina picked it up and passed it over. She unzipped it and pulled out the folders and notebook she'd kept. Names. Places. Locations. Anything she'd discovered along the way.

"One of the students at my dojo was murdered almost nine months ago. Hannah Plast. The Philadelphia police didn't find much in the way of leads. I offered everything I had. Names of everyone who attended my dojo, anyone I'd instructed privately."

She set the information on the coffee table, unsure who to give it to first. "Investigators honed in on her ex-boyfriend, Eric Reed. They believed he was the reason she was taking self-defense lessons from me."

"You didn't believe that," Cruz said.

Angie shook her head. "Hannah approached me a

week before she was..." Murdered. The word lodged in her throat. "She thought someone was following her."

"Did she go to the police?"

"No." Angie rubbed her hands on the sweatpants. "I tried to give them what little I knew. She'd mentioned a black SUV. She'd even gotten a partial license plate. I remembered her showing me the small notepad she carried around in her purse."

Her eyes burned when she remembered how frightened the young woman had been. She should've done more to protect her.

"What happened to her wasn't your fault," Quint said.

"I should've done more, made sure she was protected."

"Don't own guilt that's not yours to carry," Twitch said. He squeezed her hand.

"They arrested Eric," Angie continued with a sigh. "I tracked down Hannah's sister and got the notepad I remembered seeing."

Cruz reached out and picked up the smallest pad on the stack of things she'd set down. "Is this it?"

Angie nodded. The man flipped through the contents, paused on the last page with writing. "Did you show this to anyone?"

"I tried," Angie whispered. "The detective wasn't interested in it, said the investigation was closed."

The man's lips thinned as he passed the notepad to Quint.

"I made a few calls, to a couple of people I'd met at the dojo. One..." Angie wasn't sure how much to share. She didn't want to get anyone in trouble.

As if sensing her concern, Quint leaned forward. "We

aren't here in an official capacity, Angie. Neither of us have jurisdiction over any of this. We're here to help advise Twitch and Counterstrike on how to help you."

"One of the women in my dojo worked at the DMV. She pulled all the records for any black SUVs with that partial license plate and gave me the list."

"I'd imagine it was fairly long," Medina said.

"It is." Angie reached out and took the list out. "I started working my way down it until I came across a name. Noah Wints."

"What about him stopped you?" Twitch asked.

"He hired me for private lessons a week after Hannah was killed," Angie whispered. Fear quickened her pulse. She cleared her throat.

Twitch stood, headed into the kitchen behind them. He returned with several bottles of water. He handed one to her. She uncapped it with a grateful smile and took a sip.

"Did you tell the detective?" Cruz asked.

"He said it was a coincidence," Angie muttered. "Noah Wints is a very prominent businessman in the area. The detective said he likely heard my dojo's name on the news and decided to throw business my way."

"Which is likely what Wints would've said," Quint said. "Please tell me you didn't continue the lessons when you found out about this license plate."

"I did." Heat rose in her face. "Hannah deserved justice. There's no way her scrawny ex could have..."

The murder was gruesome... one of the worst things she'd ever seen. The detective had shown her the crime scene photos, likely in an attempt to see if she'd somehow been involved. Nausea pitched her stomach.

"What happened?" Twitch asked.

"He caught me snooping more than once but seemed to find it amusing." She swallowed. "I confronted him. He laughed it off, then threw me out. The first attack on me was two nights later. I'd just closed up the dojo and someone grabbed me in the parking lot."

"I suspect that didn't end well for that someone," Twitch said, admiration in his voice. He glanced at Cruz and Quint. "She's a black belt in four martial arts."

"I never told you I was a black belt." She looked over at the man beside her.

"It's on your website," Medina said. "Well, three of them are. You left the Krav Maga off."

Angie shrugged.

"What happened after the attack?" Quint asked.

"I filed assault charges against the guy, who was a local gang banger that claimed he was getting back at me for breaking him and his woman up." Angie paused when Cruz picked up one of the file folders and started thumbing through the contents.

She wondered what his trained FBI mind saw. Was anything she'd gathered worth a damn?

"The second and third attacks were the same. The police thought I was paranoid and determined to blame Noah Wints for everything by the time the fourth attack happened."

Cruz's jaw twitched when he looked up at her. "Four attacks in what span of time?"

"Three weeks, give or take a few days."

"Did you have any interaction with Noah Wints during that time?" Quint asked.

"Some private lessons toward the beginning, but nothing toward the end." She pulled out the file at the bottom of the stack. "The threats started between the third and fourth attack. Print outs appeared on my printers at the dojo and my house."

"Are these the originals?" Twitch asked as he looked through them.

"No, the police kept those. I filed a report, just in case it could be used later. If..." She sounded nuts. She broke off the rest.

"In case they finally pulled their heads out of their asses and started looking into Wints," Medina finished.

"What made you run?" Cruz asked. He leaned back, crossed his legs. "You fended off three attacks, filed reports for each one. Turned in all the threats. What changed with the fourth attack?"

"The attackers were always local thugs, hooligans. The ones used for the fourth were more organized, the leader called someone and ordered them to hit Claude. Then the kids. They were going to go after the kids who went to my youth center. I couldn't let that happen. Someone had already been hurt because of this."

"Who did they hurt?" Twitch asked, his voice low.

"Chastity," Angie whispered. Tears shimmered in her gaze when she looked at him. "I never knew her real name. She was a dancer who signed up for kickboxing lessons. She was in the hospital for four days, told the police it was my fault. She'd taken the lesson meant for me."

"You couldn't have known they'd go after her," Quint said. "When did she get attacked?"

"Shortly after the second attack on me." Angie swallowed. "I knew who was behind them. I just couldn't prove anything."

"But you turned everything over to the cops. That got someone scared," Cruz said. "Did they start investigating the attacks after Chastity's statement?"

"No. Shortly after that, Noah Wints was attacked in the parking garage of his building," Angie said. "He said the attacker was smaller than him but a martial arts expert."

"They suspected you," Twitch said.

Angie nodded. "I was teaching a class at the dojo when the attack happened, but they still considered me a person of interest."

"That's when you ran," Cruz said.

"They showed up with a search warrant, claimed someone had reported me for running drugs through the dojo." Anger filled her voice. "They didn't find anything, but after they left a teenager kid who hung out there told me he'd found drugs in a locker. He flushed them before they got back there."

"Convenient he found them," Quint commented.

"He admitted he'd heard that I'd been set-up."

"That's when you ran," Twitch said.

Angie nodded. "They searched the dojo a few hours before the fourth attack. It all happened on the same day. I decided to lie low a few days, let the heat settle. Then I'd come back and figure out what to do next. I went to Cincinnati for a few days."

"Is that when you were attacked outside of a bar?" Medina asked.

"Yes. At first, I didn't think it was related. but then I found a message under my hotel room door. 'You can run but you can't hide.'"

"Were there messages after each attack?" Quint asked.

"At first, yes. But that stopped after Atlanta," she said.

"What was different about that attack versus the others?" Cruz asked.

Her pulse quickened. As if sensing the shift in her, Twitch took her hand. "They're here to help. So am I."

"That's the first attack where someone died," she whispered.

Quint and Cruz looked at one another, but neither made a comment at first. The latter recovered first. "Did the attacks accelerate after that?"

"Yes."

"How did they find you?" Medina asked.

"That's what we need to figure out," Twitch said.

"Most of the warrants for you are misdemeanors. Only a couple have the potential for felony charges," Cruz said.

"Milo's sister, Jennifer, is an attorney. She's going to work on getting any charges against you dropped once we gather the evidence needed to substantiate your defense." Twitch squeezed her hand again. "We'll get this bastard."

"We need the money trail linking him to the attackers," Cruz said. "And statements from as many as we can get admitting they were hired."

"No one ever knows who hired them," Angie said. "I always asked."

"You have photos of them," Quint commented as he

thumbed through the folder Cruz had looked at earlier. "That's impressive."

"I hoped they'd help later on, but they might just be more evidence against me."

"Did you take photos of yourself? The injuries you sustained?" Cruz asked.

Angie chewed on her lip. "No."

"I'm thinking her injuries weren't that bad since she knows four martial arts," Medina said with a chuckle.

"I got lucky," Angie admitted. "None of them knew me. They weren't warned I could fight. All they saw was a woman."

"That was their first mistake." Cruz looked at Twitch. "What's the plan?"

"I'm hoping once we gather evidence you can get involved. Formally."

"That's my hope, too." The man motioned toward the folders. "Can that system you have access to use this?"

"Yeah." Medina chuckled. "HERA will churn through this in no time and pull all sorts of leads, I'm thinking."

Angie hoped so.

"While HERA is processing what Angie gathered, we'll keep her safe here. Medina and his team are putting extra drones around the exterior of the safe house. It was only equipped with interior surveillance." Twitch looked at Cruz. "She'll stay here, tucked away."

"If that doesn't work or the investigation stalls, we'll consider another strategy," Medina said.

Twitch tightened. "We aren't discussing that. Not yet."

"What is it?" Angie asked.

"Make you more visible. See what he does," Medina said.

"Bait," Twitch growled. "That's not up for discussion, not yet."

"I'll do it," she said. "I'm tired of hiding. Cowering. I want this bastard arrested. Hannah deserves justice. So does Chastity."

"Not if it puts you at risk." Twitch glared at Medina. "Let's see what we get from the information you gathered. HERA is one hell of a system. It'll pull a lot of information from the databases it's connected to."

"It will," Medina said. "Twitch, my team, and I will keep you safe no matter what, Angie. It's good to know you're willing to go with Plan B, but I'm with Twitch. Plan A will work."

Okay then. Plan A was better than what she'd had before—no plan at all.

"I'll make sure patrol cars cruise by here more often," Quint said.

Angie was humbled by how many people were helping her. How could she possibly repay their kindness? Their trust. They didn't even know her, yet they believed her.

The front door opened. Milo entered carrying plastic bags in both hands. He held them up as he moved past Angie and Twitch and entered the kitchen. "I brought groceries."

Angie's stomach rumbled.

"Let's get you fed," Twitch commented. He looked at Quint and Cruz. "You two are welcome to join us."

"I'd better get to work," Cruz said as he stood. "I'd appreciate it if one of you could send a copy of all of this to me, and whatever HERA finds. I'm going to start making some calls, seeing what I can do. Unofficially."

"I'll do the same." Quint rose.

"Thank you." Medina escorted the two men out. Angie followed Twitch into the kitchen. The two men already had half the groceries put up before she arrived. Fresh fruits and vegetables filled the hydrator drawers. Protein powder sat beside a blender on the counter by the fridge.

Milo separated boneless, skinless chicken breast into freezer bags. He grinned. "I'll pick up anything else you might want. I wasn't sure what you would and wouldn't eat."

"This will be perfect." Angie's gaze settled on Twitch as he unloaded brown rice and black beans and an assortment of other staples. "I've eaten whatever I could afford or had access to for so long I think my body's forgotten anything else."

"You can get back to the way it was before now," Twitch said as he shut the pantry.

The past few months had been bad in many ways, but the lack of a daily routine was the worst. She'd always eaten whatever she wanted within reason. The martial arts and kickboxing courses she led every day had kept her accustomed to an active lifestyle—one she'd love to get back to, even if only partially.

"How about I fix you an omelet?" Milo asked. "Anything you don't eat?"

Her stomach rumbled again. "I think I'd eat cardboard at this point."

The man's lips thinned as he moved to stand on the opposite side of the island from Twitch. The two men's gazes met. Neither seemed happy at hearing her confession. She hadn't been around protective men for a long time, but she remembered the type well enough. She'd grown up surrounded by them, thanks to her father.

"Sorry," she mumbled. "It wasn't all that bad."

"You don't have to lie to make us feel better," Twitch said as he started dicing mushrooms. "We'd rather hear the truth."

Angie nodded.

"You should call your family, let them know you're okay. I'd imagine they're worried," Milo said. "Your father's still active duty?"

"He retires in eight months, unless he can convince them otherwise. I'm not sure he's fully ready for retirement," Angie said with a smile. "I do need to let him know I'm okay, though."

"You have other family?" Milo asked.

"My younger sister Rose is a computer whiz and lives in California. I also have an older sister, Mia. She's..." Angie paused. "Complicated. All she's ever said is she went into Dad's line of work."

Twitch halted the chopping, slid his gaze to hers. "She's military?"

"She was for a short time," Angie hedged. "I'm not sure where she went from there. Dad knows more than me, but he won't talk about it."

"It bothers you not knowing." Twitch made the statement rather than ask. He cut red and yellow peppers. "We know people who could find out, if you want to know."

"Dad said I'm better off not knowing." Angie shrugged. "I wouldn't mind talking to her, though. It's been a long time." She missed her family. "Do you have family?"

Milo glanced at Twitch, who halted his chopping again.

"Sorry." She winced. "Not my business. Forget I asked. I just got homesick suddenly. My brain kicks me into different thought patterns when that happens."

"I have a twin brother and a little sister, Jennifer. She'll actually be your lawyer. Mom's still alive, but in a facility. She has cognitive issues because of the abuse she suffered." Milo's lips thinned. "She's why we started Counterstrike, using the bastard's billions."

Angie's stomach twisted into knots. "I'm sorry that happened to her. I'm sure she's proud of what you've accomplished. Thanks to you, the world is a better place. That's all we can hope to do, right? Make it a better place than it was when we arrived."

"Yeah, I suppose so." Milo cracked eggs into a bowl.

"I've got a sister, younger. She's got a kid. Ryan. He's seven, going on twenty," Twitch said with a chuckle. He glanced at Milo. "I'm gonna miss his game this afternoon."

"I'll make sure Ethan and I swing by, hang out with him and his buddies afterward," Milo said.

He'd make sure they swung by and hung out. Had Angie ever had friendships like that? She'd never been the type to make friends easily, likely a byproduct of the military upbringing where she was uprooted every few months. Even though her father had a regular base now, that hadn't always been the case—far from it in fact.

"Can I help with anything?" she asked.

"No, we've got it. Milo here is a savant in the kitchen. I'm kind of surprised he hasn't kicked us out yet."

The man smirked. Amusement glinted in his gaze. "Mari's told me its rude to keep people out of a kitchen. Cooking is a bonding experience, or so her mother says. I've discovered it's simpler to adapt to her style. It causes less arguments between Ethan and me."

Twitch chuckled. "How's it going with her in the house with you all? You're a bit OCD."

"They have their floor. I have mine," Milo said. He smirked. "We've had a few adjustments to make—mostly on my side. A woman in the house full-time wasn't ever on my radar."

"She's one hell of a woman."

The admiration in Twitch's voice incited her curiosity, but she bit back the questions perched on her tongue. Milo didn't strike her as the type to share his personal life. His gaze slid to her, then Twitch.

"My brother and I have a three-story home in Austin that we share. Our sister lives next door. At first we'd tried switching Ethan and Jennifer so that he and Mari could have the cottage to themselves." Milo chuckled. "Jennifer and I living together lasted a month."

"Surprised she didn't kill you before then." Twitch took a sip of his coffee.

"My sister is a slob." Milo shook his head and continued chopping. The swift, hypnotic movement of the knife sliced through the silence a few beats. "She's the best attorney around, meticulous with details, and obsessively organized. I suppose her home is her escape from all of that."

"My sister Rose is like that," Angie said. "It used to drive my dad crazy, but he finally learned to accept she wasn't ever going to be like him."

Twitch motioned toward a stool. "Sit. You want coffee?"

"I should probably eat first. It's been a while since I've had caffeine," Angie admitted. "I was a bit of an addict before this started."

An alarm pierced the area. Angie's pulse quickened. Both men drew their weapons and bookended her. Twitch motioned toward the pantry.

"That's not happening. I'm not cowering," Angie said. Legs braced apart, one foot behind another, she flexed her fists. "I'll stay behind you, but I'm not hiding."

"Fair enough. Let's sweep the house." Twitch looked at Milo. "You take exterior."

CHAPTER 6

Twitch cursed. The safe house was under attack. How the hell had they been found?

A drone appeared in front of Twitch. He grunted his assent when it began a slow sweeping pattern. Another arrived and got into position in front of Milo.

"Not sure I'll ever get used to these things," Milo commented.

"What the hell are they?" Angie asked.

"Surveillance drones. Part of the HERA system we mentioned before." Twitch glanced behind him. "Take my belt loop and stay behind me."

Milo exited the front door. Twitch swept the living room, then headed down the corridor. Movement to his right drew his attention.

"Stop, or I'll shoot," Twitch warned, but the person had darted out a broken window. "Northwest side, out a window."

He shouted the information in case Milo was within

hearing distance, but the drone had already given chase. Twitch moved through the rest of the house.

"You aren't going after him?" Angie asked, her voice raised. "He's getting away."

"He didn't get away." Twitch motioned toward the drone when it flew back and returned to position in front of him. "He's down. The drones are armed with a sleeping drug The Arsenal created."

Twitch cleared the last two bedrooms, then holstered his weapon. Anger kept him quiet as he put an arm around Angie and guided them into the living room. Milo stood in the entry.

The man looked outside. "He's down. I called Quint. He'll be here with a couple of units and a detective from Robbery."

"How did he find me?"

A growl rose from Twitch's throat. "Good question."

Medina entered the room. The man paused near Milo and rolled his eyes. "Z, I just walked in. Give me a second to catch up."

Twitch almost pitied the operative. "You didn't get far."

"A mile away," the man commented dryly. "Perimeter alarm was set off, but Z's saying someone tried to hack into the system shortly before that." Medina's lips thinned as his cell phone rang. "It's Zoey."

Milo motioned toward the door. "I'll handle Quint and his crew when they arrive."

Twitch nodded as he angled Angie to the sofa. Medina sat in the chair nearby.

"Twitch and Angie are with me, Zoey. Tell me you got a trail."

"The bastard is slippery and cocky," Zoey said. "He got into the first layer of security, the area we call the mousetrap. We intentionally set the first layer up like a standard system for the safe houses so the alarms would be set off quickly."

"So he was trying to turn them off? For what? An attack in broad daylight?" Angie shook her head. "That doesn't make sense."

"It was a test," the woman said. "He also left a message."

Twitch tightened. Son of a bitch.

" 'You can't protect her. She's mine.' " Anger filled Zoey's voice. "I'm forwarding the message and relevant information about the hack to Quint and Cruz. He could technically call in the FBI since HERA is protected by the alphabet soup. We'll get the bastard."

Medina clicked off. "We've secured a house two down to the left. The team and I will remain nearby. I'm calling in a second team to rotate with us."

"Not sure that's necessary," Twitch said. While he appreciated the assist, The Arsenal was burning a lot of man-hours in addition to what he suspected was an already crazy workload. "You all have been busier than hell lately."

"It'll be the orphaned operatives. They aren't on teams and most are itching to prove they deserve a spot on one." Medina chuckled. "But, yeah. Things have been nuts enough for me to earn a team quicker than I expected. Me and another guy, who'll lead this second crew. Raul. He's solid. Former DEA and CIA. Deep cover work."

Twitch grunted. He didn't need a 411 about anyone The Arsenal sent. They only hired the best, which was why he trusted them to assist when Counterstrike needed protection personnel.

"What does he mean I'm his? I don't even know him!" Angie's voice spiked. "This is nuts."

"We'll get him." Protectiveness fused with Twitch's anger when he put an arm around her. She settled into the contact as he focused on Medina.

The man's gaze swept the area. "Not sure how he tracked us here."

Twitch wished he knew the answer to the question that'd plagued him since the alarm went off. All they could do for now was move once more and see if the bastard found them again. If he did, there was a bigger problem. A much bigger one that left him wondering what the hell Angie had gotten herself into.

Quint and the SAPD took less than half an hour to process the scene and take the man into custody. Twitch doubted they'd get much from the bastard, who claimed he was confused and went to the wrong house.

Right.

Milo shut the door behind the last of the police. "This neighborhood is burned. Get her secured elsewhere. I'm going to go see what they get from our visitor, but I don't expect much."

The man didn't wait for a reply. He opened the door and left. Twitch glanced out the blinds and watched his boss leave.

"We're leaving?" Angie looked around. Eyes narrowed. "But you all put drones here."

"And whoever's after you knows this place now. One

attacker was a test," Twitch said. "You took out three armed men by yourself. Now you have us helping."

The woman paled. "The real attack will be worse."

"Let's go." He motioned Angie toward the door.

"Shouldn't we get clothes? Supplies?"

"We walk out with nothing," Medina said. He held up Angie's backpack. "All we need is here."

He'd grabbed the notes and information she'd gathered. Good. "That's crazy."

Maybe so, but it kept people safe. Twitch didn't take chances with people he protected. He pulled out the disposable cell he was using and tapped Counterstrike's number. Patch answered on the first ring.

"Hey, man," Patch said.

"Need wheels."

"Head south, corner of Kissing Oak and Iron Gate," the man said. "The Uber will take you to The Alamo. Head across the street, then down one block west. Wheels are in the first-floor parking garage of the Rivercenter parking structure. White Ford Escape. Dump the phone before you get into the Uber. Medina does the same."

"His team?"

"Once you and Angie are secure, Medina can contact his team," Patch said. "They can monitor the burned location, see if there's movement."

"On it." Twitch hung up and called up the Uber ap on the disposable. The driver was an elderly woman named Nancy. Blue Chevy Equinox. He glanced at the license plate number and the image once more, then shoved the phone into his pocket.

"Dump your phone before we get into the Uber," Twitch ordered Medina. "Your team will need to make the jump later. I need them hanging back, watching this place."

"Roger."

Twitch firmed his grip on Angie's arm and guided her toward the corner. Unease pricked his skin. He never liked the transition part of this bullshit when it required trusting unknown civilians. It was the one component of the network he didn't like.

He saw a blue SUV in the distance, but a blue truck turned the corner at a high enough rate of speed to squeal tires. His pulse quickened as he pulled his weapon.

"Get down," Twitch ordered.

Medina's voice rose beside him as he spewed orders into the com he wore in his ear. The man tugged Angie behind him as he took position beside Twitch. Exposed with no immediate cover, they had no choice but to confront whoever was in the truck. Running would get them shot in the back if it was a drive-by. Angie crouched behind them as the vehicle jumped the curbed and angled closer. It slammed to a halt.

Twitch took a few steps back, but kept his weapon trained on the vehicle as a drone appeared and hovered in front of them. Something shot out of the small device. One of the men ducked, drew a weapon.

Fuck.

"Don't even think about it," he growled. "Hands in the air or you're leaving this in a body bag. Your call."

"You're outnumbered." The man sneered when three more men exited the truck, weapons drawn. "We ain't leaving without her."

"I'd count again," Medina said.

Four men appeared from the side of the house, weapons drawn. Another drone hovered on the other side of the truck. A black SUV pulled up beside them. More men poured out, weapons trained on the gun-wielding assholes.

"Go. We've got them." Medina motioned Twitch toward the SUV. Sirens sounded in the distance.

"Get in," Twitch ordered Angie.

Fortunately, she opened the rear passenger's side door without delay and climbed in. Twitch jumped into the front seat. The vehicle pulled out and headed down the road.

A dark-haired man looked over at him, then back at Angie. "I'm Raul with The Arsenal. Are you both okay?"

"I'm fine," Angie said. "Shouldn't we wait for the police?"

"No." Anger punctuated the word as Twitch looked out the window. "If you all hadn't been here as backup..."

"We were." Raul's jaw clenched. "They shouldn't have found this place, not that quick."

"Patch was sending us to the Rivercenter parking garage."

"Change of plans," the man commented as he turned onto the freeway. Ringing filled the cab. "Yeah."

"No flight plan was filed when she left Chicago," Zoey said. "Everything was dumped before you went to San Antonio, Twitch. You weren't followed."

None of the statements were questions. Twitch kept quiet and let the woman's anger add tension to the already charged situation.

"Jesse, what the hell am I missing? How did the bastard find her?"

Silence descended a few moments as Zoey chatted with her coworker. Jesse Mason was one of the six brothers who led The Arsenal. Milo had mentioned he'd turned the team he'd led over to Levi and taken up a position within Operations to help run missions and oversee the network. From what Twitch had heard, the man was one hell of an operative.

"The only thing left in the mix is Angie," Jesse said.

"No." Angie's voice rose. "I'm not in contact with that bastard. You think I'm helping him?"

"I'm not saying that," Jesse replied, his voice softer than before. "I need you to think back to when this all started, Angie. Are there any moments of time unaccounted for? Any span you don't remember?"

"What are you thinking?" Zoey asked.

"You think she's got a tracker in her," Raul said.

"She's the only common denominator." Jesse sighed.

Son of a bitch. Someone had chipped her like an animal? How? When? Twitch looked back at her. Paleness crept across her face. Wide, frightened eyes peered back at him.

"I don't remember blacking out or losing time," Angie said. "I wasn't knocked out during any of the attacks. At least, I don't think I was."

"Were you injured? Stabbed? Struck with anything that would've cut your skin?" Twitch asked.

"I needed stitches after the second attack in Philly." Shock resonated in her voice, a shaky undertone that thickened the unease within him. "Between my shoulder blades. The knife cut deep enough to need stitches."

"We'll need the location where you were treated and the doctor's name, if you can remember," Zoey said.

Twitch tightened as Angie rattled off the information. Was she safe in the San Antonio area? Should she be put deeper into the network? While he trusted the process and its security, he didn't like the idea of sending her out there alone.

Six months.

She'd run and fought this bastard and the assholes he sent after her for six months without any help. He couldn't imagine shoving her into the network with a new name and letting her do it all over again if the asshole found her.

Raul clicked the call off. Twitch realized he'd not heard a part of the conversation. Damn.

Get your shit together. She needs your A game.

* * *

A TRACKER.

Angie sat in the back of the vehicle. Too stunned to speak, she looked around when Raul parked in a strip center. A sandwich shop was at the far end. A nail salon flashed a neon sign advertising a sale a bit farther down.

Were the men hungry?

No. Raul hadn't parked them in front of the eatery. She exited when the men did and turned to face…a tattoo shop. What the heck? Her pulse quickened as Twitch splayed a hand at her back.

"We're going to get this figured out," he whispered in her ear. "You aren't alone. Okay?"

She nodded.

A tracker.

Raul entered Sinful Tattoos. A burly man with a scruffy beard looked up from a manga he was reading at the counter.

"Fuck, man! What the fuck!" The man's booming laughter echoed within the small space. A couple men looked up from their stations further back, their glowers matching Twitch's beside her. "I thought your stupid ass was dead."

"Nah, man." Raul tugged the man into a hug. They exchanged back slaps that'd likely crack a normal person's ribs. "Dani mentioned you had a kickass setup here, man."

"Yeah." The man grinned. "Heard Dom's out. Great news. Tell him to get his stupid ass over. I'll fix up those tats he likely got while he was away."

Out. Away.

Prison.

Angie tensed. Unease coated her insides. Why had they come here?

"This is Scribe, best damn ink master around," Raul said.

"You looking for ink? I'll work you in," the man offered, his gaze darting between Raul, Twitch, and Angie. It settled on Angie.

Raul's voice lowered. "We need your back area for a while, man."

The man's gaze narrowed but remained on her. "That's not fully operational yet. Dani's girl Riley just came by with the installation crew last week. They aren't done."

Raul didn't reply. The man crossed him arms and nodded. He turned and headed toward the back.

Angie and Twitch followed the two men as they wound past the tattoo stations and through an office. Scribe opened a closet, shoved against the far wall and barreled through the opened passageway.

What the heck?

A small area opened up. Half-finished sheetrock along the right wall showed what she assumed would be a bathroom on the other side. Pipes and a toilet sat in the space. Once finished, the area would resemble the one they'd used in Austin.

Wow.

"It's not much. Wasn't opening it for use for another two months," Scribe muttered.

"Emergency," Raul said. "This is Twitch, from Counterstrike. His crew is taking over entry into the network. Scribe here is a new volunteer. This'll be a safe harbor for people to enter the network until someone from Counterstrike or The Arsenal can help them."

Angie nodded.

"It's a hell of a network. When that Riley Mason chick came in and started talking about it, I was all in, man." Scribe shoved his hands in his pockets. "Don't know Twitch here, but that Arsenal bunch is solid. They'll get you safe, girl."

Emotion clogged Angie's throat. She glanced around at the space. "Thank you for what you're doing here. It's going to help a lot of people."

"A couple people will be coming in soon. They're landing a chopper in the old Kmart parking lot across the highway," Raul said. "Send them back here."

"Will do," Scribe said. The man headed out.

"We couldn't use an already set-up place?" Twitch asked, his hands clenched.

"This was easier. Chopper lands across the highway. Easy in, easy out," Raul said. "Scribe's solid."

"You've known him a long time. I thought you were new to The Arsenal crew."

"I am." The man's jaw twitched. "Was undercover in a drug cartel for the DEA and CIA a long time. He lived in Marville, where I'm from. Helped look out for my sister. Kept my brother apprised of the situation while he was locked up for murders he didn't commit."

The man took a step forward, into Twitch's space.

"If we're done second-guessing my loyalty to this cause and my new crew, can we get Angie secured?" Raul asked.

"Don't mean it like that, man." Twitch locked gazes with the man. "I've known a couple of good men who did time for doing the right thing when the justice system screwed up."

"Then we're cool. You'll likely meet Dom down the road. Appreciate it if you didn't bring this shit up. He's still not fully settled in his head," Raul said.

"Understood."

The man motioned toward the exit. "I'll go wait for Logan outside and bring him back here."

Angie waited until Raul left. Questions zinged around

in her brain, but she didn't want to intrude. Twitch turned.

"You've got an expressive face," he said. "My cousins did time for assault. They beat up my sister's ex. She tried getting away a couple times and couldn't. I was overseas and not around to help. They tried to help but made things worse. My aunt got word to me. I phoned Ethan. He and Milo helped Bea."

Wow. The fierce protectiveness resonated within his gaze, his stance. He was the kind of man who'd do anything for the people he loved without hesitation. The strength and confidence he exuded was almost hypnotic in its calming presence because it'd been so long since she wasn't the strongest person in a room. Being able to sit back and let someone else take the lead was…

Angie looked down and tugged on her shirt, suddenly too aware of her attraction to the man. She was nothing more than a job to him, one of likely many he helped. But it'd been so long since she thought beyond survival enough to experience anything beyond fear and worry.

"It sounds like you've got a really close family," she said, unsure what else to say.

"We have our issues. Every family does," he said. "What about you? We'll get you in touch with your family so they know you're safe. I'm sure you're wanting to talk with them."

"They have enough worries without me adding mine."

"That's not how family works." He took a step closer. "Three months is a long time to go without knowing how you are, especially for a man like him. I'm thinking your dad would want to know what's going on."

He would. He'd drop whatever he was doing and be at her side, barking orders and kicking butts until he got things resolved. "I can't endanger him."

Chastity's attack had fractured something inside her. She couldn't let someone she loved be harmed by Noah Wints. Even though she'd seen recent pictures of Claude and the neighborhood kids on the dojo's website, she still worried. Had they been attacked? Were they safe? Guilt already plagued her that Twitch and everyone else at Counterstrike and The Arsenal had put themselves in harm's way for her.

"You could've been killed today," she whispered.

"We had the situation under control." Twitch ran a hand down her hair. "This is what we do, Angie. We're good at it."

"What if he keeps finding me?"

"Then we put you deeper into the network where he can never find you. You'll be safe. No matter what we have to do, this will end." Determination thickened his voice. He caressed her jawline near her chin. "Is that why you aren't calling your dad? You don't want him in danger."

"He'd be right here in the middle of everything."

"That's his call to make. It's not my business, but I can tell you I wish Bea would've told me what was going on so I could've gotten her the help she needed." He pulled his hand away.

"She didn't want to worry you."

Twitch looked away when the entryway opened and Raul came through with Logan and a woman with spiked purple hair with pink tips. The latter carried a laptop, which was open.

"Hey, Angie." Logan smiled. "Are you doing okay?"

"A bit freaked about the possible tracker."

The doctor reached into a bag and pulled out a scanner of some sort. It looked a lot like the wands airport security used. "Let's see if we can figure out what might be happening. Raise your arms up at your sides."

Angie assumed the search position. The doctor grinned, but didn't comment as he moved the device around her. It remained silent along her left side. Then her right.

"Her back, Logan," the woman said. "That's where she was stitched."

"Angie, this is Zoey, aka Zero D," Logan said with a smirk.

"Oops." The woman glanced up from the laptop she held in one hand while typing with the other. "Sorry, I'm normally not the rude, growly one. This whole thing has me thrown for a loop. I've never, ever thought about having to scan people for trackers. What kind of sick psycho chips people?"

"Bree and Rhea chipped all of us," Logan said.

"That's different," Zoey clipped. "You're all crazy commandoes who are constantly in the crosshairs of crazies. Of course we're tracking you. We do it out of love. This psycho chipped Angie like she's his possession."

A growl rumbled from Twitch.

"Don't growl at me," the woman said. "You're thinking the same thing. I bet Angie is too."

"I was." Angie tightened when the scanner beeped from where Logan stood behind her.

"It's there, isn't it?" Twitch asked.

"It appears so," Logan said. He glanced at Twitch. "I'll need a better area to work with, somewhere she can be comfortable."

"Scribe's got an open station you can use. We can close the curtains and stand outside to keep everyone away," Raul said.

"The curtains will be enough," the doctor said. He put a hand on Angie's shoulder. "I'm going to need to get this out of you, okay?"

"Please do." She didn't even care how much it hurt. "The sooner, the better."

"Don't pull it until Cruz and Quint are here. I want them witnessing it for the investigation." Zoey glanced over from her laptop. "They're on the way over from the former safe house."

CHAPTER 7

"Cruisers are patrolling the area more frequently," Quint said. He looked around at the north San Antonio housing division. "This is a quiet neighborhood. That should help keep her secure. If you need anything, let me know."

"Appreciated." Twitch shook the man's hand and waited until he got into his vehicle and headed out. Then he shifted his attention to Cruz. "There a reason you're hanging around?"

While Twitch appreciated the help Cruz and Quint were giving, it'd been several hours since they'd left the tattoo shop. He wanted to get Angie settled so she could rest.

"We should chat," the man said. Arms crossed, he glanced back at the closed door of the two-story, three-bedroom house where Angie was. "I've contacted Philadelphia police. They've forwarded their investigation notes so far—for Hannah's murder, the attack on Chastity, and the attacks on Angie."

Cruz's grim expression made Twitch's stomach sour. "Something's wrong."

"The work's solid," the man said. "They dug into Noah Wints's financials and found nothing. He even turned them over without argument, said he was willing to help however they needed."

"Either he has nothing to hide, or he's hidden it so well he thinks he's invincible." Neither option left Twitch feeling good about Angie's situation. "Hopefully the tracker we got out of her gives us a lead."

"The FBI's looking into the serial number. I spoke with the Philadelphia office. They're sending someone to speak with the staff on duty at the time Angie went in," Cruz said. "I should hear something later today, assuming they got ahold of the doctor who stitched her up."

Twitch knew The Arsenal had gotten the serial number from the device before the FBI took it into custody as evidence. They'd likely hunt the doctor down and get some answers before the suits Cruz sent could. Knowing Zoey she'd likely already hacked into the hospital's surveillance footage and records from that day.

"That woman in there's taken one strike after another for six months straight. A person can only handle so much."

"I've been thinking the same thing," Twitch admitted.

"If you want, I can try and find her a youth center or somewhere to teach a class. I know a few in town that have programs. I'm sure they'd love having her volunteer, even if it is only once."

"She'd probably appreciate the opportunity," Twitch

said. "Let me know what you find out. I'll chat with her about it and get a security plan organized. Thanks."

"Anytime."

Twitch headed inside once the man left. Angie sat on the loveseat staring at a muted television. A national newscast played, but he doubted she was paying attention. Her dark brown eyes were glazed over.

He sat on the seat beside her and waited until she shifted attention his direction. "How are you doing?"

"I've been better." A weak smile appeared.

He draped an arm around her waist and sighed heavily when she sank into his embrace. Head against his chest, she set a hand on his stomach. Milo would kick his ass if he walked in and saw, but Twitch didn't give a damn.

"You've had a hell of a day," he said.

"So have you."

"You've had a lot of them nonstop. Cruz is going to try and find a youth center or some other organization you can volunteer at, maybe teach a class or two." He caressed her arm and studied her startled face a moment.

She was beautiful. Full lips meant to tempt a man. Round, expressive eyes. In any other circumstance he'd carry her into a bedroom and make them both forget about the shitty day. He suspected Angie would be an active, passionate lover—the kind who drove a man wild.

Fuck.

Angie licked her lips. Need settled in his dick.

"Is that safe? Teaching a class?"

"You don't have the tracker anymore, so it should be. We have enough coverage to keep you safe," he said. "Your emotional wellbeing is just as important as your physical safety."

He tried to imagine what it'd been like for her the past six months. Would he have functioned as well as her? Probably. But he'd been trained to adapt and survive. She likely had as well.

Twitch met several folks who'd been raised by a career military parent. Most had a regimented mindset that preferred routine. He doubted an on-the-run lifestyle allowed much in the way of routine, especially for someone as active as Angie had clearly been.

"I'd love to teach a class," she admitted. "I'd even settle for going to a gym."

"We'll find you something. How's your wound?"

She sat up and patted the bullet wound. "I cleaned and bandaged it this morning. It's healing great."

Twitch smiled. "I meant the one on your back. Is it hurting?"

Her skin tinged a cute red. "Oh. That wound. Sorry, I guess I have a few."

"I'm hoping we can avoid you getting more." He ran his finger across her arm. "You're cute when you blush."

She licked her lips again. He tracked the flick of her tongue, felt his body ache in response. Yeah, he was totally screwed when it came to Angie. He'd be smart to admit the attraction, tag Chatter in for her protective detail.

But he wouldn't.

Twitch refused to let anyone but him protect Angie. "So?"

"So what?" Her gaze remained on his face. She licked her lips again.

"The wound." He leaned closer. Their hot breaths melded. Lips a couple inches from one another, he stroked her cheek and added. "Is it hurting?"

"Not much." She touched his face. "You're feeling it too, aren't you? The attraction."

A smart man would say no, but he didn't want to lie to her. "Yeah."

"We shouldn't explore it. That wouldn't be good, would it?"

"It'd be the best thing that's happened to me in a long while, but no. It wouldn't be good." He ran his thumb across her lips. "Your safety's the only thing that matters right now. I won't risk it."

Twitch needed a distraction for them both or he'd pick her up and take her to bed. He couldn't imagine anything better than laying her out like a feast and savoring.

"I should phone my dad and let him and my sister know I'm okay," she said. "He'll likely send a battalion, a few dozen tanks."

Twitch chuckled. "Let me chat with Zoey, see what we can arrange."

"Thank you." She stroked his face. "For everything."

* * *

Two days later...

"You're sure this is safe?" Angie asked. She stared at the laptop sitting on the coffee table in front of her.

It'd been two quiet days since the last attack. She and Twitch had settled into a comfortable routine of doing very little. She ate regular meals and rested. A lot. They watched movies and chatted.

The more she got to know him, the more she was drawn to him.

"It's the safest connection we can make unless we take you to The Arsenal," Medina commented. "Warning, though. We had to establish contact with your father to make sure he was secured on his end, so he knows you're calling."

Her stomach somersaulted. He wasn't going to be happy she'd kept him out of the loop about everything. "Did you tell him what's going on?"

"No, that wasn't our place," he replied.

Angie nodded and looked across at Twitch. She'd grown accustomed to him sitting beside her, so it felt a bit awkward for him to be farther away. The afternoon had rushed by far quicker than she'd expected despite there being nothing to do.

Twitch had found movies on television. She'd stretched out on the sofa and watched, mindless to everything else going on around her. The reprieve from the worries was exactly what she'd needed.

Classes.

She hoped Cruz got something worked out for her to teach a course somewhere. Honestly, she'd be just as happy at a boxing gym or anywhere she could work off some of her energy.

"We'll be back here if you need anything," Medina said as he stood and moved to the other side of the room where Twitch was. "Just so you know, Zoey and the other geeks are on the com. You won't hear them, but they'll hear the conversation. It's routing through The Arsenal so HERA can maintain the line's security."

She nodded. Everyone already knew everything. She had nothing to hide from the people keeping her alive. She clicked the green button to activate the call.

It'd been a while since she'd seen her father—nine months. A smattering of gray hair along his temples was larger than she remembered. The fine wrinkles around his eyes and mouth had darkened and moved farther out.

"Dad." Emotion clogged her throat and burned her eyes. She clutched her throat and silently willed the blockage away. Her father wasn't big on emotional breakdowns. They'd all had plenty of those when Mom passed.

"Angel Eyes." The man blinked rapidly. "I've been worried. I got your message six months ago, then the few emails after that. Are you okay?"

"I'm okay. I'm safe for now."

"Yes." His lips thinned. "I'm looking forward to hearing how you came to be associated with The Arsenal. They're a solid organization. You know I've never been a fan of privately run groups in the military theater, but they're good."

Angie swiped at the tears trekking down her face. "I'm sorry I haven't called. I-I didn't want to take the risk my calls were being tracked somehow."

"What's going on and how can I help? I've got a lot of time accumulated. Tell me where you are and I'll head there on the first plane." The man paused. "The Arsenal's in Texas. Are you there?"

Angie glanced up at Twitch, who shook his head. "I'm safe, Dad. An organization The Arsenal is affiliated with is helping me. Someone's trying to kill me. I'm not sure who or why. We have suspicions, but the authorities are looking into it."

"Do you need money?"

"No, Dad. Really, just talking to you is all I need. I miss you. How are Rose and Mia?"

"Rose is worried. She's still in California trying to convince that group to fund her virtual reality programming idea. You know how she is when she gets into her work. Entire weeks go by and she doesn't notice," he said with a bluster. "She's worried though. It'd ease her mind to see you, chat. If that Arsenal crew can establish a contact, I can get her to a base there in California. Same setup we're using on that end."

"We'll see what we can do in a few days," a voice Angie didn't recognize said. "We need to see how the investigations are going before we risk contact with her sisters. You're a more secured asset, sir. Her sister wouldn't be. It could put Rose at risk."

"I understand. Do what you think is best, Edge. You and Quillery are the best damned support personnel I've ever worked with. I trust you to keep my girl safe. Whatever you need, you let me know."

"We will."

Silence descended a few beats. Angie swallowed the worry in her throat. She didn't want Rose or anyone else in danger because of her. Would her dad be okay? "Dad, have you heard from Mia?"

"Not since the last time we spoke. She'd mentioned going on a long-term mission, though. Your sister can take care of herself. I don't much care for the organization she'd tied up with, but she assured me this was her last assignment. Then she'd look into other avenues."

Angie tightened. She remained silent, but her dad's lips thinned. He'd seen her tense.

"I know we've heard that before, but she's serious this time, Angel Eyes."

"I hope so. I worry about her. And you. How are you doing?"

"I'm fine now that I know you're secure. If that changes, you let me know. Whatever it takes. I'm in. Okay?"

"I love you, Dad. I'm okay." She glanced up at Twitch. "I'm not sure how long we should have this connection on, so I'd best let you go."

"Stay safe. Listen to Edge and Quillery. They're first rate."

"I will," she promised, even though she had zero idea who Quillery and Edge were.

She clicked off before she lost the courage to. Ending a call with her dad was harder than she expected. Tears spilled out from her burning eyes. She swiped at them and kept her gaze down.

The sofa dipped with Twitch's weight as he sat beside her. His clean scent enveloped her nostrils when he drew her close. "You could've talked for longer."

"He knows I'm okay. He'll let Rose know." She sniffled, and looked up at Medina. The man shifted his stance. "Who are Edge and Quillery?"

"They're Zoey's bosses. They designed HERA," Medina said. "Your father has likely worked with them in the past. They are both focused on another situation. Actually,

Quillery is supposed to be on maternity leave, but that's not working very well for her or Edge. They're both neck deep in diapers. They're husbands are, too."

"Jud is changing diapers?" Twitch laughed. "I'd pay to see that."

"You should ask him about delivery day." The man chuckled. "He was a wreck."

Twitch took Angie's hand and squeezed. "Jud is the only man who's ever knocked me on my ass. They showed up back when Ethan's fiancé, Marisol, was having some troubles."

Angie smirked.

"What he isn't telling you is that Jud's scrawny twenty-year-old nephew was there and darted both of them with a drone. They were out for a solid half hour." Medina crossed his arms. "It was before my time, but I've seen the footage."

"That better not get to the Counterstrike crew," Twitch warned, amusement in his voice.

Angie appreciated the two men trying to lighten her mood. She was glad her dad knew she was okay. Hopefully she'd get a chance to see him and Rose soon.

Twitch's cell chimed. He picked it up off the coffee table. "Cruz found a youth center who needs a teacher for their self-defense class. Teenagers. Tomorrow afternoon."

"That's perfect," she said. "Please thank him for me."

Twitch typed something and then looked up at Medina.

"Uh oh," Medina said. "You've got that look on your face."

"What look?" Angie asked.

"The one my buddy Fallon gets right before he blows something up." Medina crossed his arms. "I take it we aren't waiting until tomorrow to get her out."

"Milo scouted out a kickboxing gym owned by someone he knows. Said it wasn't too far from here," Twitch said. He glanced at Angie. "You up for a drive?"

"Yes!" She blurted the response with enough force to make Medina chuckle.

The man turned. "I'll let my team know. If you two are sparring, I might need to record it. You know, just in case."

Anticipation and excitement filled Angie. A kick-boxing gym wasn't exactly her thing, but she'd do anything that got her out of hiding mode.

* * *

TWITCH BOUNCED ON THE BALLS OF HIS FEET AND WAITED for Angie's next strike. Sweat dampened both their skin, but he wasn't about to tap out. Joy glinted in her gaze as she feigned an upward kick, then swept his knees.

Pain ran along his back when he impacted with the mats. Amusement echoed from the sidelines where Medina and a couple of the Arsenal operatives watched. A drone hovered near the entry to the small training area they'd commandeered at the kickboxing gym.

He'd started off trying to take it easy on Angie because of her injuries. The three days recovery had clearly helped because she was kicking his ass.

Hard.

"Damn." He rose and grinned. She'd yet to use the

same move to take him down. Anticipation pounded within his veins, a surge of adrenaline and arousal he couldn't ignore. "You aren't taking it easy on me, are you?"

"Was I supposed to?" She laughed. Her long, black hair bounced around in its ponytail as she shifted her stance. "You're good."

"Angel, you're kicking my ass."

"Maybe, but I'm having to work harder than I've worked in a long time to do it." She turned and snagged a water bottle from beside the mats.

Appreciation resonated within her gaze as it raked over his body, pausing briefly on his exposed chest. Twitch hadn't removed his shirt to show off, but his muscles flexed beneath her perusal, much like a peacock strutting.

Sweat glistened off her skin. The snug shorts she'd gotten from the gym's apparel store hugged her firm hips and accentuated her well-toned legs. Legs that'd wrapped around him many times since they'd started sparring.

Twitch smiled, proud that he'd held his own with Angie as long as he had. He'd never gone up against someone smaller than him who could best him once they were down on the mats. His size, brute strength, and training typically gave him a win every time.

Until now.

"Where'd you learn your floor techniques?" Twitch asked.

"My sister." She took another drink of water, then capped the bottle. "She makes me look like a yellow belt."

Damn. Twitch smirked. "Remind me never to piss her off. You're more than I can handle."

"Oh, I don't know about that." Angie approached as he took another gulp of water. "You're handling me pretty well. Better than anyone in a long while."

Blood surged to his dick.

Twitch shifted his stance and hoped the loose shorts he wore hid the evidence of his arousal. He'd remained focused on the sparring until now, but without his competitive side activated, the lizard part of his brain had kicked into gear. Suddenly, he wanted to take her to the mats for an entirely different reason.

"I like it," she whispered. Intensity resonated in her gaze when she looked up at him.

"Like what?" He lowered his voice, glanced over at Medina, who'd remained but had remained a ghost since they'd arrived.

"You didn't pull your punches. You gave as hard as you got. I like that you didn't hold back."

She wasn't wrong. He'd done his best to win, except for one small exception. "I avoided your left side. Other than that, I did my best to take you down. Damn proud I'm still able to walk around. You're one of the best I've gone up against."

She smiled. "You're pretty good yourself."

"Come on. Let's get showered and changed, then I'll take you to eat."

"Thank you." She touched his upper arm and smiled. The beauty struck him center mass. "Thank you for giving me this break. I hadn't realized how much I missed it until I was here."

He'd bring her here every day if it earned him a beautiful smile every time. "You should do it more often."

"Do what?"

"Smile." He stroked her face. "It's the most beautiful thing I've seen in a long time. Come on. Let's get showered and changed before Medina over there loses his patience."

CHAPTER 8

Angie peered at the small white and brown building they'd parked nearby. Teenagers milled about near a set of double doors. "Are you sure this is a good idea?"

"You need a distraction, a recharge." Twitch undid his seatbelt and shifted to face her. "Today, we give you a small piece of your life back."

Awareness arced between them when he squeezed her arm. Angie nodded and undid her seatbelt. Her stomach pitched. "I'm more nervous than I realized."

Twitch's sexy dark gaze narrowed. "If this is too much too soon, I'll take you back home."

"No." She shook her head. "I just… I don't want to disappoint them."

"That's not possible," Twitch said.

"You haven't even seen me work."

"Angel, you kicked my ass for hours yesterday. I've seen your work firsthand."

Angel. Heat rose in her cheeks when she thought of the gym yesterday. Sparring with Twitch had been the most fun she'd ever had going against someone. Not only had he held his own, but he'd won a couple of the skirmishes.

"You can kick anyone's ass." He smirked. "Besides, this is a youth center, not a black belt only dojo."

Anticipation hummed within her as she exited the vehicle and kept her gaze on the cluster of kids, most of whom watched Twitch as though they were about to bolt. She couldn't blame them. The man was taller than anyone she'd ever met and thick with muscle. He exuded confidence. He not only projected that he could kick anyone's ass—he screamed he'd do so without a problem.

The longer Angie spent around the man, the harder it was to deny her attraction. Twitch closed the distance between them and settled a possessive arm at her waist as his gaze focused on the huddled teenagers. The move marked her as his—a fact she would normally be irritated at. But it set a protective tone, one Angie welcomed she knew was supportive rather than intrusive.

Twitch knew she could defend herself—he just wanted her to know he'd help when needed. She'd learned the hard way the past few months that strength didn't come from standing your ground and fighting your battles. It came from being smart enough to realize when help was needed and being confident enough to ask for it.

"Hey," Angie said.

"Yo." One of the teenagers approached. He looked Twitch up and down. "You the instructor tonight? No way I'll ever be as big as you. One punch and you'd knock anyone on their ass."

The kid was scratching five two and was rail thin. His

clothes didn't hang as loosely as most Angie had worked with in Philly. His hat, shirt, and gear were all red and black, likely gang colors of some sort since most of those around him wore similar markings.

Either they were young recruits or surviving in a gang-heavy environment by blending in. Neither option left Angie feeling good about their chances. Too many got lost between the cracks when well-meaning organizations sometimes caused more problems than they solved. Kids like this needed more than a few classes a week.

Angie kept her thoughts to herself as they came to a stop in front of the kids, who all kept their gazes on Twitch—the obvious threat. She almost laughed at being so totally ignored, but she suspected the man beside her would be difficult for anyone to take down.

"I'm just here to watch," Twitch said. "Angie here is the expert. She'll be working with you tonight."

"Pffft." One of the girls looked Angie up and down. "Shit, I could take her. I'd rather learn from you." The sexualized tone crackled tension within the air as Twitch tightened beside her.

"She kicked my ass yesterday," Twitch said with a grin.

"No shit?" One of the kid's looked them both up and down. "Damn."

"Let's head inside," Angie ordered.

"Whatever." One of the kids turned and opened the doors. Everyone surged in.

"Don't run," an older man shouted. Most of the kids slowed. A few didn't. He shook his head. "Every day. Seems like they'd learn by now. You must be Angie. I'm

Wallace, but most everyone calls me Wally. Mickie had a lot of great things to say about you. So did Mack."

Angie didn't know Mickie or Mack, but smiled and shook the man's hand. "Thanks for letting me help out."

"I'm afraid they were a little barren on the details of what you'd be doing tonight. Our normal instructor has been on medical leave the past couple of weeks. Honestly, anything would be better than what they've had lately—which is nothing but an empty room with mats." The man motioned toward the room. Mats were stacked up along a far wall. A few chairs were set out along the farthest wall. "There aren't any fancy uniforms or gear or anything."

"That's fine. I believe in training people in everyday clothes when I can. It gives them familiarity with movement in a realistic, situational environment."

The man's eyes widened. "Well, Chuck has them pretty broken into karate moves and a few other things, so don't let them trick you into thinking they don't know anything. Some of those boys are bigger than you."

"I'll handle my own. If I get into trouble, Twitch here will help me out."

Twitch chuckled. Wally's eyes widened. "He sure is a big one. I'll be in my office if you need anything. I suspect Mickie and Mack will show up soon. They asked if they and a couple of friends could observe."

"Great."

Angie looked down at the snug yoga pants and T-shirt she'd found inside the dresser. They weren't exactly the best clothes to meet people in, but she'd worn worse. At least they were clean.

Angie kicked off her shoes and set them alongside the

massive pile of assorted sneakers and footwear. The kids set out the mats, connected the Velcro and fanned out within the room. Eagerness danced within their twitchy limbs and curious gazes when she stood in the middle of the room rather than toward the front of it.

"Let's start with a warm-up. Who'd like to guide everyone in what you normally do?" Hands darted up within the room. She pointed at one of the smaller girls. "We'll start with you."

The girl air pumped her fist a minute as shouts and cheers echoed around her. Angie hung back and observed the group, noted the shyer ones on the edges toward the back. A couple of the larger boys intentionally encroached on one smaller girl's personal space.

Angie was impressed with most everyone's form. She adjusted a few as they went through the typical warm-up routine for a karate-based class. While karate was great at instilling confidence, she'd never personally found it helpful for kids raised in a streetfighter lifestyle. It might help, but it wouldn't achieve a mind shift change. Not alone.

Once the kids were warmed up, she paired them off to practice what she assumed was Chuck's primary focus. It took longer than she expected for a few to accomplish the more involved methods, which gave her a much better indication at where the class, as a whole, stood.

"Okay. Form a circle," she ordered. She stood in the middle and waited as the kids obeyed. A few wiped their sweat-filled brows. A couple others went to the side of the room and drank from a water fountain.

Angie made a mental note to bring some bottled

waters next time. She'd handed out water mugs with her dojo's name in Philly. She wished she had something like that right now. The kids needed to stay hydrated.

"Okay, I want to do something a bit different with the rest of our time. Let's talk about street fighting. Specifically, how to get away from a confrontation against a bigger and stronger opponent. Or several of them." A few of the smaller kids' eyes widened. "Size doesn't dictate the victor."

"It sure as fuck doesn't hurt," one of the bigger kids said.

"Let's see. Come up here."

"No way. You'll kick my ass. I ain't stupid." The kids around him shoved him forward.

Angie motioned for one the smaller shy girls toward the back to come forward. The girl's gaze widened. "Come on up. It's okay."

The girl's shoulder's hunched in as she gingerly moved to Angie. Red rode in the girl's face. Angie put a hand on her shoulder and squeezed. She kept her attention on everyone else. "It's not easy feeling confident in a large group of people. Walking around, never knowing who'll jump out and start something. We can't always turn and leave."

"Damn straight. We don't run," one of the guys said. "That'd just make the beatdown worse later."

Several others nodded.

"What if I told you that you can prevent someone from challenging you without doing anything?" Angie looked around, noted the skepticism. She motioned toward Twitch, who stood at the edge of the mats. Several women hovered nearby. "How many of you would take him on?"

Everyone laughed.

"What about you?" She directed the attention at the bigger kid she'd pulled up.

"No way. Guy's huge?"

"Is that the only reason?" Angie motioned Twitch forward. Eyebrows raised, he moved forward.

She took a moment to appreciate the man's stealthy grace, the confident stride. The kids parted when Twitch arrived at the huddle. Amusement flickered in the man's gaze. A broad grin quickened her pulse.

"Are you about to kick my ass, Angel?"

"Maybe." She let the laughter fall around them a few moments. "Okay, let's pretend Twitch here is shorter. Smaller. Would you mess with him?"

"No way," the kid beside her said.

"What's your name?" Angie asked the boy.

"Manuel."

"Yours?" She ran her hand down the girl's back.

"Theresa."

"I'm going to show you all how someone Theresa's and my size can defend themselves against larger people, like Manuel and Twitch. The fight starts before the first punch is thrown." She looked around, then pointed at a few of the kids near her. "Don't ever stand with your legs together. Keep your feet apart, preferably one foot slightly behind the other."

"Why?" Manuel asked.

"Balance. If I were to shove you and your feet are together you'd be thrown off balance and stumble backward. You'd lose a defensive position. But let's say Twitch came up to me right now and pushed." Angie raised her eyebrows and grinned when the man shook his head.

Anticipation rolled through her when he closed the distance and looked around at the kids. "I'm about to have my ass handed to me."

Twitch pushed her, hard enough for her torso to lurch backward. Good. He wasn't going to take it easy on her.

Angie didn't move.

"No way," Manuel declared. "You didn't go back."

"Because my feet were apart and one foot was behind the other enough to keep my center mass balanced," Angie said as she motioned to her feet. "Also, I can strike immediately and get away. What would you do?"

"Kick his balls," one of the guys said.

"That'd work, but if he's quick enough," Angie said as she raised her foot up toward his crotch. Twitch's eyebrows rose as he grabbed her foot. "Now he'd yank me down and I'd fall. That won't help me get away."

"So what do I do?" Theresa asked. "I don't run fast cause I'm short. They always catch up."

They always catch up. Angie's stomach soured. Manuel's jaw twitched. The boy crossed his arms and regarded the girl standing beside him.

"You scream," Manuel said. "Make sure someone hears you. That's what Chuck says."

"Good. You scream but keep distance between you and him." Angie pulled back from Twitch and motioned toward his knee. "Your knees, legs, and elbows and fingers are your best weapons. Your attacker's knees are the best place to hit if you want to slow them down when you start running. Kick the knee as hard as you can. He'll either fall or be hurt and slowed enough for you to run away. Always kick with your back leg."

Theresa's eyes widened. She nodded fiercely.

"That's when you'd either run or strike a second time. If he leaned forward, punch his face with an upward thrust of your flat palm to the bottom of his nose. Hard." Angie looked at the girl. "Do that only if you can without taking extra time getting into position. You're hitting hard, but fast. Then running like hell."

"What if he grabs you?" one of the girls asked.

"How?" Angie asked.

"By the throat. Both hands." Theresa gripped her throat.

Twitch's jaw tightened when he looked back at the girl. Angie took the man's hands, guided them to her throat. He firmed the grip enough to emit gasps from the kids watching. She smiled her appreciation for his assistance.

"You want to strike before the grip constricts your breathing. Take both your hands, bring them up between his upper arms and push outward. This should break the contact because he won't expect you to fight back. The best way to knock his ass away long enough to run, though, is to take your hands, put them at the back of his head, right above the neck. One hand atop the other. Yank his head forward and slam the upper part of your head into his nose. It'll hurt, but I promise it hurts him more."

Some of the kids laughed when Twitch jerked away like she'd struck him.

"You've got to hit with this part of your head, though.

Anything else and you'll hurt yourself." She motioned toward the upper part of the crown.

"What if there's more than one?" Theresa asked. "Wh-what if one has you from behind and the other…"

Jesus.

Angie wondered what the hell Theresa went through on a regular basis.

"Show her, let her do it," Manuel ordered. "Greg, get your ass up here. We need a second."

Theresa backpedaled. Angie put an arm on the girl's shoulders. "He's right. You doing it will help."

Manuel moved to stand behind the girl. Eyes wide, she whirled to face him, but he turned her around. "Easy. You're gonna learn."

Both the boys were much larger than the girl, whose unease was genuine enough to set the proper tone. Everyone huddled closer.

Angie glanced back at where the elderly man leading the center had wandered. She'd gotten in trouble for being too real with teenagers back in Philly when she'd volunteered at a few places.

"What?" Manuel asked. He tracked her gaze. "He won't come out. He never does."

"Okay, then we're gonna get real here. There are a lot of ways to get away from these holds. I'm gonna show you the most effective, which causes the most hurt." She looked around. "The goal is always to get away, but sometimes that means hurting the one who wants to hurt you. These aren't used to attack someone."

"We get it," Manuel said. "Show her."

She hoped she wouldn't get into trouble with Cruz or

his friends, who'd put in a good word for her to volunteer here. But the kids wanted to learn. Clean fighting techniques didn't always save someone from real life troubles because things got dirty—which meant you had to get dirtier.

"Let's do this."

* * *

SWEAT DAMPENED HER SKIN BY THE TIME THE KIDS HAD LEFT the building. The two-hour training had gone four by the time she'd gotten everyone's questions answered. The kids had bonded and worked together to learn. The smaller, more frightened students opened up toward the end and asked pointed questions and set up real-life scenarios.

Scenarios Angie had handled before at her dojo. It was one of the reasons she liked working with women and children. What they learned helped them in real life.

"That was awesome." A curvy woman with light brown hair typed on her cell phone as she and a black-haired woman approached with a blonde holding her upper arm. "I'm Mack. I'm with Daxton, but you haven't met him yet. He's a Texas Ranger, which you may not know what that is since you aren't from Texas. He works with Cruz and Quint sometimes. They're good friends. This is Mickie. She's with Cruz. And the gorgeous blonde is Corrie. She's with Quint."

Uhm… wow. The woman had gotten it all out in one breath without pausing her texting. "Hi."

Mack glanced up. "Cruz told us to be cool and not

approach other than to say hi, but I don't think he knew you were like a ninja version of Wonder Woman. We got to talking and we'd really like it if you could show us some of what you just did with them. Except, you know. For adult women. Just us for now, though we all know some people who could benefit from learning real techniques. We've taken self-defense courses, but I dunno. I don't think half of it would really work well enough to get me away."

Angie blinked. Twitch chuckled as he arrived at the huddle. He handed a bottle of water to her.

"You're huge," Mack said, her eyes wide. "What are you? Six four?"

"Six five," he said.

"Damn." The woman peered up. "We haven't met. I'm with Daxton. You know him?"

"Yeah, he's helped us out a few times." Twitch took a drink of his water, then looked at Angie. "You did great with them."

"I'm sure a few of their parents will disagree when they run home and tell them what they learned today," Angie said.

"Hardly," Mickie said. "They learned more today than they ever have here. Thank you for doing this. Cruz mentioned you owned a dojo in Philadelphia. That's so impressive."

"I've enjoyed working with the women and kids. Today was a lot of fun. It's been a while since I've held a class." Angie bit her lower lip. How much had Cruz and Quint mentioned to the women?

Mack and Mickie looked at one another. Heat rose in

Corrie's cheeks. Angie shifted her stance and took a large drink of the water Twitch had given her.

"Quint and Cruz mentioned you were having some trouble. I guess that's why Twitch here is with you. I assume you're with Counterstrike?" Corrie asked. She held her hand out, near Twitch but not as close and Angie expected.

She tracked the move, noted the woman's gaze hovered in Twitch's vicinity, but not directly on him. She didn't make eye contact, yet, seemed to.

Twitch took the woman's hand and shook. "It's a pleasure you meet you. Quint's been a huge help to us, so have Cruz and Daxton. They're great guys."

"They are." Mack lifted her phone and shook it back and forth. "So, we were thinking we could hang out tonight, maybe learn a few things from you. I'd suggest my place, but Daxton just said you likely wouldn't want Angie leaving the safe house. So we can meet you all there. I'll bring snacks. The girls can bring drinks and whatnot. If you're in." She paused. "Angie?"

In for what?

Self-defense for them. Right. "Sure. Assuming that's okay with Twitch." Was it okay? Was a safe house secure if a bunch of people knew where it was?

The man's jaw flinched a few beats, but he nodded. "Let's find somewhere else."

"Okay, big man. Got it. I'll sort the location and text everyone the place and time. I'll get your number from Ethan or Milo, Twitch. I'm sure Daxton has their contact info." Mack grinned and hugged Angie tight. "It sucks that you're here because of why you're here, but I have to admit I'm glad you are. We've wanted some real defense lessons for a while now. Just wait until you hear what all this crew's been through—and you likely will. A couple drinks and one of us will likely start oversharing. It's kind of our thing."

"Come on, let's let Angie rest. She's bound to be tired after that class." Mickie offered a smile. "We'll see you tonight."

Angie waited until the three friendly women left. She kept her gaze on Corrie, who was quieter than the other two.

"Corrie's blind," Twitch offered.

"No she isn't," Angie argued.

Twitch chuckled. "She is. A chiropractor. Ethan was talking about her one day."

Talk about impressive. Angie imagined the woman overcame a lot of challenges to do what she loved. She was looking forward to chatting with the woman more. They had a lot in common.

"Mack wasn't wrong," Twitch said. "Those women have been through a lot from what I've heard. The guys don't talk about it much, but they've shared enough with Ethan for us to see why they're willing to help Counter-strike, even when we don't color fully inside the lines."

Angie wondered exactly how far outside the lines the organization went when necessary. From what she'd seen so far, they were capable of just about anything. "Thank you for sticking around. I'm sure it was pretty boring."

"On the contrary." Twitch turned to face her. "You're one hell of an impressive woman. You waded straight into those kids' fears and smashed them into bits. More importantly, you bonded them. Did you see the way Manuel and his buddies were walking Theresa and the smaller ones out? They'll look out for one another."

"That's always the hope. Break the cycle of violence by building the community." Angie walked alongside Twitch as they headed toward the vehicle. "My methods aren't exactly… typical."

"I noticed. Mack's right. The shit you teach will work without question." Twitch smirked. "It'll also mean broken bones and concussions at the least. But it'll work and get the victim safe."

"They aren't victims. That's an ugly word." Angie thinned her lips. "Are you sure tonight is a good idea? I'm kind of surprised we did this today."

Twitch glanced around, then focused on her. He ran a hand across her arm. "You've been on the run a long time. Alone. Normally we would keep you isolated, but there's no logic behind that. Not with you right now. Getting a piece of your normal back for a while will help more than keeping you secluded."

"I enjoyed today," Angie admitted. "It just feels weird to not be constantly on guard."

"You are though," Twitch said. "You're honed in to your surroundings regardless of where you are. Between that and The Arsenal team watching the perimeter, you're safe. You may as well see to your mental happiness a bit. It's hard to fight an enemy if your morale is depleted."

"You're right. Speaking of depleted"—she looked up at him and patted her stomach—"I'm starving."

CHAPTER 9

"So what's Twitch's deal?" Mickie asked. Her eyes widened. "He's intense."

"Like Cruz isn't," Corrie teased. She wiped her brow with a hand towel and collapsed on the sofa. "That was the most fun I've ever had getting my ass kicked."

Angie chuckled at the women as they all fell where they stood. Mackenzie, Mickie, Corrie, and their contingent of friends. There were so many she'd given up remembering everyone's name. All that mattered was they were all very friendly and she was having more fun than she had in a long, long time.

It felt strange to be relaxed. A psychopath was chasing her around the country. But Twitch was right about her morale being depleted. She hadn't realized how much so until today—when she'd gotten a slice of her normal back.

"Of course he's intense. Some idiot is trying to kill Angie and he's tasked with keeping her alive," Mack said. She peered up from her cell phone. "Remember how

Daxton and Cruz and Quint and everyone else was when we had our situations?"

Angie shivered remembering the women's harrowing experiences. They'd shared the past several hours as she trained them on more advanced self-defense tactics. Each of them had done a phenomenal job learning the maneuvers. She hoped they'd never be needed.

Her gaze roamed to the corner, where Twitch chatted with Cruz and a very handsome Texas Ranger, Daxton Chambers. Both of the latter had watched intently while Angie worked with their women. They had the same protective auras as Twitch, and their love for Mack and Mickie shone brightly with their playful banter.

"Who are you texting?" Mickie asked.

"Penelope. I'm telling her about the foot to the hip and leg wrap around the neck to flip the big dude move. I want her to try it out on Moose." Mack looked up. "Weird. She's not answering me."

"She doesn't need ninja moves to kick someone's ass," Mickie commented. "Penelope and Moose are a couple friends of ours, firefighters. You know, we should have a barbecue, invite everyone over. It'd be good for Angie to meet more people. What do you think, Cruz?"

Before the man could comment, his cell chimed. Daxton's did as well. Both men glanced down, then over at Twitch.

"Moose just texted," Daxton said. "They're at a fire."

"At the youth center," Cruz added.

No. No. No.

"Let's go." Twitch settled an arm around Angie's shoulder when she stood.

"We'll let you know what we find out," Cruz said as she and Twitch headed out the door.

Angie jumped into the vehicle and clicked her safety belt on. Her heart thundered hard in her chest as Twitch pulled out and onto the road. He clicked the phone icon on the display panel, then punched Medina's name.

"What's up?" Medina asked.

"Fire at the youth center," Twitch replied. "I'm getting Angie secured. Cruz will let us know what they find at the site, but we could use a couple people there, taking pictures. Assessing the crowd, in case the bastard's behind this and someone's watching."

"On it." The man disconnected.

He was getting her secured? Angie grabbed Twitch's arm and squeezed. "We're going to the fire."

"No. We aren't." He looked over. Streetlights spotlighted his face. "Angie, what could we do once we get there?"

Dread filled her gut as she peered at the city whizzing by. Nothing. She'd be just as useless there as she had been the past several months.

"We don't even know this is connected to you," Twitch said.

"It'd be mighty weird if it wasn't. I don't believe in coincidences, not anymore."

"Agreed, which is why getting you to the safe house is my priority."

"I shouldn't have come tonight," Angie commented. "Today was a mistake."

"No." Twitch took her hand. "You needed a break, a reboot on your mindset. You aren't running any longer."

Angie kept quiet as they pulled into the safe house's garage. A shiver ran along her spine as she followed Twitch into the house. Weapon drawn, he cleared the entire house. She remained behind him, fingers interlocked around his belt loop even though he hadn't told her to.

Twitch holstered his weapon and guided her into the living room. She sat on the sofa and ran her hands along her upper arms. His phone chimed.

"The center was empty. No injuries," Twitch said. "Cruz will let us know once there's more information."

Angie nodded. No injuries was good. The phone thudded against the coffee table. Twitch sat beside her and wrapped an arm around her.

"Don't. I stink." She leaned away from the contact.

He ran a hand down her braided hair. The tension eased in her. She closed her eyes a moment and focused on the soft glide of his hand, from the top of her head to just past her neck, along her upper back. Then up again.

She rested her head against his chest and draped her arm along his waist. The man was solid muscle and warmer than a heating blanket. Did he comfort all the women he protected like this?

"What was that thought?" Twitch asked.

"Nothing."

"Nothing doesn't tense you so fast your entire body moves." The stroke along her hair halted. He caressed her cheek with his other hand, then used two fingers to lift her chin. Their gazes collided. "You're safe."

"I know." She swallowed and looked down. "I was just wondering how many times you've had to do this. Calm freaked out women." *Let them latch on to you like you are the only thing holding them up.*

"You aren't freaked out, not in the way we typically see. Your situation is different than our normal cases," Twitch said. "I don't handle many of those. Like I mentioned before, my size is an issue for a lot of the women."

"You're gentler than most men I've met," Angie said. "I'm sure they realize that in time."

"Most are processed through quickly. They need Jennifer's legal expertise and counselors. Some need career development training and job placement. We give them the tools they need but try to remain as hands off as we can so they acclimate to a new normal. The drones The Arsenal gave us make that way easier."

"I'm sure a few of the people you help latch on," Angie said. "I've had a few like that."

"It's hard not to let them." Twitch sighed. "I think of my sister every time a new client shows up at our offices. Whenever we get a call. The kids break my heart."

"How old was your nephew?"

"Four, almost five." The stroke returned, a gentle glide along her head, down her back. "Bea finally got the courage to leave when the bastard went after Ryan."

"It's not easy breaking the cycle, asking for help. Mom was raised in a violent home. It was one of the reasons my dad insisted we all know how to defend ourselves."

"Your mom passed?"

"Heart attack, ten years ago," Angie whispered. "It feels like yesterday. She was our heart. Dad says that's why she left us too soon… he used up her heart too fast."

"That's not true. You know that, right?"

"For him it was. He wasn't the same after she passed, like he died too." Angie peeked up at the man looking down at her so intensely. "I avoided relationships a long time after she passed. I couldn't imagine taking a hit that hard. It wasn't worth the risk."

"And now?" Twitch caressed her face. "Is it worth it?"

"Seeing Mack and Daxton and Cruz and Mickie together tonight, hearing the other women talking about the men they love... yeah. I think it'll be worth it. Onc day. If I get through this Noah nightmare."

"You'll get through," he promised. "Whatever it takes, I'll get you through."

"What about you?" She pushed up to sever the physical contact some. "Is there anyone in your life?"

"No, though my mom wishes otherwise. She's anxious for more grandkids and doesn't think Bea will accommodate anytime soon, which leaves me on the hook."

Angie smiled. "What about your dad? Is he... around?"

"No. He cheated on Mom when she was pregnant with Bea." His jaw tightened. "She threw him out. Seven months pregnant and in a town where she didn't know anyone. No job."

God. Angie couldn't imagine. "How did she get through it?"

"Cholo's mom. My dad's sister. She showed up on my mom's doorstep one day and didn't leave until Bea was crawling. She helped Mom find a job."

"That must've been hard on them both."

"It was. Cholo's family wasn't happy she'd gone against her blood, but she didn't back down. I learned a lot from them both, about how to stay true to what I believe." His dark gaze twinkled. "You remind me a lot of them. Your fiery grit."

Awareness pebbled across her skin and arrowed arousal through her. She'd always found strong, courageous men attractive—which was why her attraction to Twitch had been almost instantaneous. The peek into his life, what'd carved him into the incredibly protective and brave man he was, though, increased her desire.

"Not sure I like reminding you of your aunt and mom," Angie admitted. He tightened against her. She splayed her hand on his chest and straddled his powerful thighs. Their hot breaths collided when she leaned forward. "I'm not feeling very familial with you."

Her pulse quickened as she closed the scant distance between their mouths and brushed her lips across his. Eyes open, she peered into his dark obsidian gaze and hoped she hadn't read him wrong—that the attraction was one he felt as well. She draped her palm against his cheek and ran her thumb over his lip.

He drew it into his mouth, nibbled a moment, then clasped her head. A shockwave of pleasure ignited within her when he took control of the kiss. He nipped and licked along the seam of her mouth, then began a carnal exploration that pooled need between her legs.

A strong hand gripped her ass, tugged her forward until she ground against him. The prominent bulge beneath his cargo pants left no doubt the attraction was mutual.

Eyes closed, she drank in the cinnamon flavor of his

mouth. It'd been too damn long since she'd tasted a man, been inside the shelter of someone's arms.

Lost in the sensations, it took a moment for Angie to note the tension cording Twitch's muscles. She pulled away, looked down. His gaze was latched on to...

Angie leaned backward, but Twitch's hand kept her locked against him. A drone was hovering within a foot of them.

"What the fuck?" Twitch clipped. The man's cell phone rang. He clicked answer, left it on speaker. "If that's you, Patch, I'm kicking your ass into the next century."

"Please don't. I don't want to train a replacement," Zoey said. "Figured you'd rather find out via me and a drone. You're about to get company."

"You could've just called." Twitch sighed and ran a hand through his hair.

"Yeah, no. I've got a badass commando of my own, you know. You boys ignore phones when things are hot and heavy."

Twitch clicked off without comment. The drone whizzed back toward the corner it'd vacated. Angie moved to unseat herself fully from him, but he clasped her thigh.

"Angie."

"Don't. I understand." She licked her lips. "Later."

* * *

MILO WAS GOING TO KICK HIS ASS.

Twitch rose when a knock sounded at the door. He

adjusted his pants, somewhat thankful Zoey's heads up had given his dick time to calm. Fuck.

He glanced back at the beautiful woman trying to pretend the world hadn't just rocked beneath them with that kiss. No woman had ever affected him so quickly. Hell, had anyone ever taken the lead and initiated a kiss with him?

Cruz and Quint stood at the door. Eyebrows raised, they both smirked when Twitch glared.

"Can we come in?" Cruz asked.

Twitch turned and headed inside. Angie rose from the sofa. Her wide, expressive eyes were almost enough to draw attention from her well-kissed mouth.

Almost.

Quint chuckled. "Sorry to come by so late, but we wanted to give you both an update on what we've found out so far. We noticed Medina and a couple of others who we assumed were Arsenal operatives milling about, snapping pictures of the crowd. We didn't want to expose them."

"Appreciated."

At least someone had their damn heads thinking about the right objective. Twitch's body was thinking with the wrong head entirely right now. Damn. Heat spread through him when he sat on the sofa and Angie settled against him. Hand on his thigh.

Unashamed they'd been caught necking on the couch like two hormonal teenagers.

Twitch put an arm around her and waited for whatever the men had discovered. He hoped the fire had nothing to do with Angie, but he doubted either of the men would've come over this late at night unless it did. He glanced at the time on his cell phone.

Fifteen minutes until midnight.

"It appears Angie's lesson at the youth center today started a bit of a revolution amongst the kids," Quint said. Amusement softened his gaze when he looked at Angie. "Do you remember a young girl named Theresa?"

"Yes. She..." Angie leaned forward. "Is she okay?"

"She is now," Cruz answered. "Apparently whatever happened in your class spurred some action within the two rival gangs, because of her. Someone suspected abuse and acted on that suspicion."

Twitch grunted. "Manuel."

"His older brother is second in command of a rival gang that Theresa's father runs," Quint said. "Manuel's stayed out of the gang, mainly because his big brother doesn't want anyone else in the life."

"My God. Are they okay? What happened?"

"The Diablos hit Theresa's house, where they found the girl fighting off two of her father's men. He was passed out in the living room." Quint's fists clenched. "Manuel defused the situation, convinced his brother and the other Diablos to keep the two men incapacitated while he phoned the police. They were arrested for attempted rape of a minor. The father and everyone else in the house were arrested for possessions of controlled substances with intent to distribute and a string of other charges."

"How does that circle back to the fire at the youth center?"

"The South Side Raptor's lieutenant got wind of his

leader's arrest and how it went down. Talk on the street pointed to the youth center," Cruz said. "To you."

"Me?"

"Apparently, you inspired Manuel to stop looking the other way, to see Theresa as someone who needed his help rather than the enemy's daughter. The boy's not in the Diablos, but he's got enough clout with the neighborhood to cause problems for the gangs," Quint said. "The South Side Raptors pipe-bombed the center to warn everyone away."

"Reasserting their control," Twitch commented.

"That's horrible." Angie paled. "The kids are all okay?"

"Yeah." Cruz shook his head. "Not sure what the hell you did in a few hours that no one's accomplished in months, but the kids are a united front right now. They're at the youth center raising volunteers for cleanup. The place is still smoking and they're already figuring out how to rebuild it."

"I need to go down there," Angie said. She rose from the sofa.

Twitch snagged her hand and dragged her back to sitting. "You aren't going anywhere."

"I need to be there, Twitch. Don't you see how dangerous this is? They're trying to do the right thing, but they're going to get themselves killed. Blood doesn't run as thick, not when gangs are vying for territory and control." Angie shook her head. "I saw this in Philly. It's not good."

"She's right," Quint said. "But so is Twitch. This didn't have anything to do with whoever's after you, but he's clearly watching the area. You showing up there could be the exact scenario he's planning for."

"And Twitch and Medina and his team are going to be there. So will you two and the SAPD. I'll be safe. Those kids aren't. They need to know someone will help get the youth center back up and running. They don't need to take this fight on alone. They need to be kids and not try to dissolve two gangs."

"Change doesn't happen overnight," Cruz said. "But it's also not your fight, Angie."

"It is. I started this. Even if I didn't mean to, I started this."

"No." Quint shook his head. "You inspired them, but Manuel started this when he did the right thing to protect Theresa. This is the neighborhood's fight. Not yours."

"But the neighborhood needs to know there's a fight. They need to know there's someone there to help."

"They'll know." Twitch grabbed his cell. "But not tonight. I'll get ahold of Milo, see what he and Ethan can do. We'll get a plan in place, one that'll keep you safe."

"I'm not hiding at the safe house." Angie crossed her arms. "The Raptors can't see the neighborhood cowering after that hit."

"It'll wait until morning," Twitch said.

He admired Angie's fighter mentality. He doubted there was any challenge she wouldn't face. But he couldn't let that compassion and determination put her at risk.

"Units will patrol the neighborhood heavily. SAPD has a cruiser staying at the center," Quint said.

"That'll help," Twitch said. His cell chimed.

Two teams inbound to youth center. Will disperse within neighborhood. ~Z

"The Arsenal's sending a couple teams to patrol the area," Twitch said. He typed a thanks to Zoey and set his phone down. "That'll give us time to strategize."

"The neighborhood's got to raise themselves up," Cruz said. "Help is good, but they've got to lead the effort so it'll stick."

Twitch knew the man was right, but he also suspected Angie wouldn't be okay with taking a backseat in the cleanup effort. He stood, kept his focus on getting her situated for the night. A plan would take several hours to form. "Thanks for the heads up. We'll circle back in a few hours. Milo and Ethan will know what to do."

He waited until the men had been gone a few moments. He activated the security system's night surveillance and then he headed down the hall Angie had wandered down. She stood in front of the master bedroom windows, gaze latched on to the inky night beyond.

Staying away would be the smart choice, but he couldn't deny the magnetic draw that commanded he find her. He drew to a stop against her back and touched her upper arms. Even though he wanted to draw her into his arms and kiss her until their worries no longer occupied their minds, he knew that couldn't happen.

"I'm attracted to you, Angie," Twitch whispered. "But I can't put you in danger by getting distracted."

"I know." She leaned against him, rested her fingers atop his on her left arm. "I understand. I shouldn't have kissed you like that. I'm not sure what I was thinking."

Twitch suspected she was thinking exactly what he'd been trying to ignore. Their attraction was too strong to avoid. "How long has it been?"

"Nine... no eleven months," she admitted. "Longer since I've had anyone that really mattered. I've never made friends easily."

"You moved around a lot as a kid?" Twitch guessed.

"Yeah. Dad was stationed just about everywhere, or that's what it felt like." Angie glanced over her shoulder. "Relationships are even harder for me."

"You don't want to get hurt. I get that. I've been the same way a long time." He roped his right arm around her waist and kissed her hair. "Then Marisol entered our lives."

Angie tightened in his arms.

"That's Ethan's fiancée. Ethan had a rough go in the service. He almost died. Things got better when he got into Milo's team, but a part of him was lost in the hell he survived."

"That happens a lot. Too many lose pieces of themselves. Some never even realize it," Angie said.

"They know. They're just programmed to believe it doesn't matter."

"That's even sadder." Angie looked up at him. "Is he better now? Because of Marisol?"

"Yeah. Seeing their love made me realize it might be worth the risk." He sighed and admitted the rest. "But it was seeing Zoey and her man that really shifted my mindset."

"How so?"

"She designed the network used to keep people safe.

One of the girls she protected…" He paused. "Her father abused her. Impregnated her. Zoey got her away, but toward the end she got taken. Tortured. Watching Gage see her through the recovery—their love conquered every obstacle. A few of the others at The Arsenal are the same way."

"I want that one day. I'm just too scared to try," Angie admitted. "Or I have been."

"You're an amazing woman, Angie. You can do anything you put your mind to."

"So can you." She turned. "I'm sorry that I distracted you tonight. I don't mean to make your job harder than it needs to be. I appreciate everything you and Counter-strike and The Arsenal are doing for me."

"I regret nothing about the kiss except that it ended." He ran his thumb across her lips. "I can't remember the last time a woman took the lead and made a move on me. That was hotter than hell."

"You're a hard man to resist." She smiled up at him. "When this is over, I want to explore this attraction."

"Me too."

"Though, I'll warn you…" She splayed her hand on his chest.

His heart thudded beneath her palm. Blood surged southward when she dragged his head down with her other hand. Hot breath fanned along the shell of his ear. A shiver ran through him. He growled but fought back the urge to haul her closer. Or carry her to the bed.

"I'm not crying out 'Twitch' when you're inside me." His cock ached as his entire body responded to the soft graze of her teeth on his earlobe.

"Fair enough. My real name is John, John Stanz. I'd love to hear my name from you." He nibbled her ear. "Call me John as much as you want, darling."

CHAPTER 10

A blackened shell stood where the youth center had once been. Angie battled the rage back as she followed Penelope through a cleared section. Volunteers, mostly from the community, worked alongside Counterstrike and Arsenal personnel. Off-duty firefighters from Penelope's division directed the cleanup while Quint and other off-duty police helped.

Mack, Mickie, and the other women she'd met yesterday had set up a drink station with cold bottled waters, sodas, and snacks. Several people dropped off eats at the area before checking in with a tall, handsome name named Moose.

Penelope's man.

Angie stifled the grin that threatened whenever she looked at the miniature donkey plodding alongside the woman. Smokey brayed whenever the woman wandered off too far. He set his boot-covered feet wherever Penelope stepped.

So cute.

"That ought to do it." Penelope leaned over and taped down a yellow flag. "There. We should be clear for Ethan's crew to do their thing."

Ethan's crew was a demolition company he'd contracted hours ago—one that'd come with enough equipment to level the entire neighborhood. Angie looked over at who she thought was Ethan. Or was that Milo?

Penelope followed her gaze.

"That's Milo."

"How the hell can you tell?"

"The dragon. Ethan's is red. Milo's is green." The woman shrugged. "I can't take credit. Marisol pointed it out to me the first time I met them." The woman patted Smokey. "You're good with them. The kids."

"They're good kids." And they were. They'd pitched in and done the bulk of the heavy lifting of the debris before the demolition crew took over. "I was too far away to hear what Ethan said. What's the plan? Are they rebuilding?"

Penelope chuckled. "That man never chooses the easy path, not when others benefit from the more challenging one." She pointed at the three-story building across a large parking lot. "That's the new community center, or will be once everything's done. This is a basketball court. I think."

That explained why so many people were inside the three-story structure. Angie watched as Twitch and another man carried large piles of things from the building and tossed it onto a growing pile.

"Wow, that's impressive," Angie mumbled. It was hard not to admire the way Twitch's muscles bunched and flexed. His skin glistened in the sunlight—a fact that she noticed because he and several of the men laboring in the building had removed their shirts.

News vans parked alongside the narrow road drew her attention. So far, she'd avoided them, mainly because Twitch and the other operatives never let the cameramen stray near her. Unease pricked her skin, though. She didn't want to get caught on video.

"You're pretty impressive, you know. Coming out here despite everything happening." Penelope paused her progression back to the parking lot. "Mack mentioned you were having troubles. If you need anything, let me know."

"Thanks."

Angie followed the woman as she headed toward the three-story building. Moose smiled and closed the distance. The two shared a brief kiss. The woman turned and smiled.

"This is Angie."

"Ah. Yes, I heard all about you this morning after Penelope here practiced a move Mack taught her via text." The man air quoted the word practiced.

Angie chuckled. "I had nothing to do with that."

"Well, for the record," Penelope said with a grin, "it worked beautifully."

Red rose in the man's cheeks. He was a couple inches shorter than Twitch, which meant he was a solid foot taller than Penelope. The two were adorable together.

"We'd like you to come by the station some time, if Twitch says it's okay," Moose said. "We're all thinking we should firm up our self-defense techniques."

Angie imagined firefighters encountered many situations where they could be necessary. Although police were typically called at the same time, emergency situations tended to be very fluid from what she'd seen.

And she'd seen far too many since her troubles began.

Twitch came to a stop beside her. Arm at her back, he smiled. "You hungry?"

"Always," she admitted with a pat on her stomach. "I smell something very good."

"Burgers. Hot dogs. Chicken. Just about every meat imaginable." Twitch motioned toward the smoke pluming up from the side parking lot of the red building. "Jennifer wanted to have a meeting with you."

Jennifer. The lawyer.

Her stomach pitched as Angie nodded and waved goodbye to Penelope and Moose. San Antonio was the friendliest city she'd been in so far—mainly thanks to Cruz and his massive entourage of friends. A few people she didn't know greeted her by name as they passed.

She hovered closer to Twitch when they halted at a picnic table sitting beneath a massive oak tree. A tall, gorgeous woman with dark hair stood next to Ethan, whose red tattoo peeked out from his polo shirt.

"You got away from the media," Twitch commented with a chuckle.

"It's Milo's turn." The man motioned toward the picnic table. "Angie, I believe you met Zoey, aka Zero D, briefly the other day. She's one of the brains behind The Arsenal."

"And I'm Jennifer, aka his annoyingly brilliant little sister." The woman held out her hand. "And your legal counsel."

"And I'm Ethan, Milo's brother. I'm sorry I didn't

introduce myself earlier when I arrived," Ethan said. "I needed to focus the media on what we wanted them to see."

Angie wanted to hug both of the women for all they'd done for her. Her eyes burned, but she forced back the emotions rising in her and shook Jennifer's hand. She sat beside Twitch as Ethan and Jennifer sat on the other side.

Zoey closed her laptop and looked around. "Who's up first?"

Ethan chuckled. "We've had a few developments we wanted to fill you in on, Angie. We also need a few questions answered to guide a few…" The man glanced over at Zoey. "…things."

Things was pretty vague and made Zoey's gaze narrow.

"First of all, thanks to Zoey and her associates, we were able to get enough surveillance footage to substantiate self-defense claims for Cincinnati, Atlanta, and the one charge in Philadelphia." Jennifer paused when Cruz arrived at the table. "Oh, great. I wasn't sure if you'd be here or not."

Angie breathed a sigh of relief. Three charges dropped was a great start. "Thank you. That's wonderful news."

"Raleigh is a problem. Although we have substantial evidence proving it was self-defense, the district attorney there won't drop charges until there's either an ongoing federal investigation or until Philadelphia verifies our assertions," Jennifer said.

"That's crazy," Zoey said. "You didn't tell me that. There's video of the attack. What else do they want?"

"He's claiming Angie's defense was more aggressive

than necessary, and therefore, refuses to drop the charges. That, in itself, is not a problem, though. I doubt he'd find enough people for a grand jury to indict." Jennifer looked at Angie. "But we've come up with an alternative plan, one that'll strike the heart of this problem."

"Which is?" Angie asked.

"This is where I share what I found, I guess. I'm thinking there's a secondary portion I'm unaware of." Zoey's gaze darted between Jennifer and Cruz. "I was about to find a trail that brings all the payments we've traced so far back to the same funding source."

"Please tell me it's Noah Wints," Twitch said.

"I wish we could. HERA is still digging into the shell corporation, but so far we've yet to find a human being behind the snarling mess." Zoey shook her head. "I hate to say it, but this bastard is slippery."

"Angie, The Arsenal has enough clout within the federal arena for their findings to be usable by the FBI. They've contracted with us on multiple occasions," Cruz said.

Angie's pulse quickened. "You're saying you can get involved. Officially."

The man met her gaze. "We can. We just need you to come in and file a formal statement."

"What about Raleigh?" Angie looked at Jennifer. "Would I get arrested for what happened there?"

"I'm hoping to defuse the situation before anything like that happens," Jennifer said.

"So am I," Cruz said.

"We have a plan B in place if Cruz's supervisors push for an arrest on the out-of-state warrant," Ethan said.

"That'd only happen if the Raleigh district attorney presses the issue, which he shouldn't because the charges have been dropped down to battery—which is only a Class 2 misdemeanor. Out-of-state warrants are rarely a problem unless they're felonies," Jennifer said. "What's this plan? You didn't mention it to me."

"That's because you'll disagree with it." Ethan smiled. "Three media outlets from San Antonio and several from Houston, Austin, and Dallas have enough b-roll footage from myself and Milo attributing today's endeavor to Ms. Bierman. We may have also alluded to her… situation."

"The media?" Jennifer spat the words. "Tell me you weren't that stupid."

"Please." Ethan shook his head. "In today's social media climate, this is a slam dunk. A woman on the run from a psychopath and a screwed-up justice system more determined to put her behind bars than help? The story practically writes itself."

The man wasn't wrong, but Angie hated feeding the vultures. She didn't want any part of a media frenzy. She looked at Jennifer. "What would you do?"

"Give the statement. Trust Cruz to handle the rest while Twitch and everyone else keeps you safe." The woman closed her leather folio. "I wish I could say we'll clear this up quickly, but from what Zoey's found about Mr. Wints, he's rich. That'll slow an already slow process down."

"His money won't stop us," Zoey said.

"Why's that?" Angie asked.

"Well, first. Milo, Ethan and Jennifer here have ten

times more at their disposal. Second," she paused and gave Cruz a suspicious look. "Second, mistakes happen."

"Zoey..." Ethan warned.

"What?" The woman shrugged. "I'm just saying we never know what'll happen. Like, a mysterious virus could hit his bank and zap all his money away for a week or... I dunno. Ever? Shit happens."

"Now I see why you suggested I skip this little discussion," Cruz said with a laugh. "Let me know what you all decide. I'm leaving before anything is said that I'd be obligated to act on."

Angie was grateful the man had already done so much. She had no doubt he'd helped facilitate discussions with the other cities. She reached out and touched the man's arm as he turned to leave.

"Thank you," she whispered.

"I've forwarded the contact information to Ethan for the Philadelphia office," Cruz said. "I'm glad we were able to help you with this."

"Philadelphia office?" Angie shifted her attention to Twitch, then Ethan. "We're filing the statement in Philadelphia? Why?"

"Because it's time we shift from defensive tactics to offensive," Ethan said. "We're taking you home. You'll meet with the Philadelphia Police Department and the FBI."

"You're running point on this now instead of Milo?" Twitch asked.

"Milo needs to stay near Austin. He's more familiar with our active clients there than I am." Ethan glanced at

Angie. "I volunteered to help Twitch with this case and get you home."

Home.

"You think there's enough to prove he did it?"

"I think there's enough to rattle cages and get someone nervous," Ethan said. "We'll leave in the morning. Medina and his team will help with the protective detail."

"So, we'll chat on the plane in the morning. Until then, enjoy the picnic and relax." Jennifer stood. "By this time tomorrow, we'll have all the charges against you dropped. Hopefully you're back to your normal life within a week or two."

Angie couldn't believe what she was hearing. Was it really over?

She hoped so.

* * *

TWITCH WAITED UNTIL JENNIFER LEFT THE TABLE. CRUZ was across the parking lot helping Mickie and the other women dole out food. Fists clenched, he looked down the table at Zoey.

"Tell me there's a Plan C," he said.

"Of course." The woman rolled her eyes. "And a D and an E and probably and F and G I don't even know. And that's just what Jesse and I came up with. Billionaire badass here likely has more he hasn't shared."

Ethan chuckled at the billionaire badass. The description fit. Twitch smirked.

"What's Plan C?" Angie asked, her voice low. Concern flashed across her face.

"Sometimes it's best if people don't know the alternative plans." Zoey's eyes widened. "Plausible deniability. It's your friend."

The woman was certifiable, but if she kept Angie safe, Twitch was fully on board with whatever the plan was.

"Why don't you take Angie over to get a plate of food," Ethan said to Zoey. "Twitch and I will be there shortly."

Fuck. Twitch offered a curt nod. Zoey glanced between the two men. Eyes rounded.

"Okay, but don't go throwing stones from a glass house or anything." The woman stood. "Just saying. You two might be badasses, but I've got commandoes of my own who'd gladly kick your ass if I told them to. I don't even think they'd ask me why they were doing it."

Angie's eyes widened. "What's going on?"

"Nothing. Come on." Zoey patted Angie's back. "I'll go introduce you to my man. He's around here somewhere."

"Do I want to know what Zoey was referring to?" Ethan asked, his gaze darkened.

"Probably the same thing you're about to say." Twitch rested his forearms on the picnic table. "Go ahead. Say it. I'm assuming there's a secondary reason you're tapping in on this and Milo's taking a backseat."

Unlike Ethan, Milo didn't interact with the clients easily. He kept to himself and rarely offered glimpses into their private lives. The fact that he'd done so with Angie had surprised Twitch.

"Angie's a remarkable woman." Ethan paused. His gaze followed the two women. "This part is hard on Milo. He's the most protective of us."

Twitch grunted.

"He's drawn to her. She's not our average client," Ethan said. Hands on his hips, he chuckled.

Twitch wasn't surprised Milo was drawn to Angie. She was a beautiful, intelligent, and capable woman. She'd halted their progression and looked back. Hands fists at her sides, gaze narrowed, she looked like she was about to pummel someone. "Not sure I'd win against her," Ethan commented.

"You wouldn't." Namely because Twitch would kick the man's ass if he so much as touched her. "Let's get this over with so I can get back to my job."

"Is that what this is? Your job?" Ethan looked around. "She shouldn't have been here yesterday to begin with."

"That's where we'll agree to disagree, boss. She's a competent and capable woman who's had a shit life for six months because of some asshole targeting her. That kind of life wears even the strongest person down. I'm not sure how she lasted as long as she did."

"That's true."

"Counterstrike protects more than a person's physical wellbeing. Or, I thought we did."

"We do." Ethan smirked. "I can see your point. Either way, you're close. Milo thinks you're too close."

"Then Milo needs to get his ass over here and say it himself instead of hiding behind you." Twitch glowered at the man near the chow line. "He thinks you'll back his play. Are you?"

"What do you think his play is?"

"Tagging in someone else for her protective detail," Twitch said. His gut clenched at the idea. He didn't want anyone else protecting Angie.

"I get it, man. You know I do." Ethan's voice lowered. "When Mari was going through her shit, I would've leveled any of you if you'd tried to step in and take over. She was mine to protect. I knew that the moment I looked into her eyes and saw her terrified determination."

"Then why are we having this conversation?"

"Because Milo's right, too. He's concerned enough to tag me in because I've been there. He hasn't." Regret flashed across his face. "I almost fucked up at the end, when shit got real and every second counted. I wasn't thinking like the protective operative. I was a man worried about the woman he loved. That could have gotten her killed."

"It didn't."

"It could have. Are you okay with that? If something goes down, are you okay with the situation going sideways because you hesitate for a second when you can't afford to? Or you're distracted?"

Twitch realized in that instant Ethan knew about the kiss. He looked away. "I can't get sidelined, man. She… she means too much. I know that's fucked up because we just met."

"I get it. You know I do."

"How did you know? I doubt Zoey told you."

"Patch reran footage, was trying his hand at the drones," Ethan said. "He's worried you'll get hurt. There's nothing holding her here when the dust clears."

"I'm a big boy. I can sort that shit without you."

"Are you sure?" Ethan motioned toward the parking lot as a blue SUV pulled up. "Hazard got your message, dropped by and picked up your family like you asked."

Twitch had sent a text to the Counterstrike guys. It'd been a long time since Bea and Ryan had fun at a gathering. Being around a lot of people would be good for his shy nephew. "It's not like that, man."

"Keep telling yourself that." Ethan chuckled. "For the record, I hope I'm wrong."

"About what?"

"About there being nothing here for her once the dust clears. We're taking her to Philly tomorrow. To her home. Her dojo."

Tension corded within Twitch's body. He hadn't expected it to happen so quickly, but should've realized Jennifer wouldn't mess around. "I'm glad she's getting her life back."

Even if it didn't include him.

"Walking away from temptation isn't easy, especially if it's more than surface-level." Ethan stood and motioned toward where Hazard, aka Joe, was with Twitch's family. "Go spend time with your family. Philly could take a while. Medina and his team will go up there separately, establish a perimeter without contact."

Twitch grunted. It was a smart move, one that'd give them two levels of protection for Angie.

Ethan slapped him on the back. "There's enough coverage here for Angie to be safe. I just hope you know what you're doing. Introducing her to them could have fallout when she leaves in the morning."

He'd known her for less than a week. Why did the thought of her leaving tomorrow upset him so much?

She mattered.

He wanted to explore the attraction they had. The connection.

He hadn't felt it with anyone in so long that the idea of walking away without trying was...

"Another thing. I'm putting Hazard with you. With Medina and his team on perimeter only, you need another man helping you with round-the-clock. The hostilities will likely escalate when we get to Philly, especially if the Feds step in."

Marisol's brother, Hazard, had tapped out of service and come to work for Counterstrike so he could be closer to his family. The man was one hell of an operative who fit in well with the crew.

Ethan's logic made sense. Twitch kept his mouth shut and forced the argument back. He wanted Angie protected, and he had been more distracted than he typically was.

"Understood," Twitch said.

"Great. Let's go eat."

Twitch headed toward where he'd last seen his sister and nephew. A nephew who was on Hazard's shoulders. What the fuck? The boy's excited laughter rumbled through the area when the man swung him up and caught him midair. Bea stood beside them, eyes on the man rather than her son.

Fuck.

Twitch recognized the look on his sister's face. Fortunately, Hazard was ten times the man any of Bea's exes were. But that wasn't saying much. The bar had been set below sea level in that regard. Twitch's, on the other hand, was on the moon. She deserved a man who could hang the damn thing in the sky.

"Uncle John!" Ryan squirmed out of Hazard's hold as soon as his feet landed on the ground. He vaulted forward and struck Twitch head on.

"Hey, Ry. How's it going?"

"Awesome! We had blizzards from Dairy Queen. I didn't even have to share! Hazard got me my own."

The man chuckled and flashed an apologetic glance to Twitch. "It was a small. I didn't realize the sugar would hit that quick."

"Why don't you go with Uncle Ethan and get some real food to balance out the sugar." Twitch motioned toward the food area as Ethan approached. The man picked Ryan up and headed off.

"Are you sure this is safe?" Bea whispered. Her gaze darted around the area. "Erm. You're still at work. Right?"

"Yeah." Twitch kept his attention on Hazard. "Thanks for bringing them."

"No problem." The man's gaze roamed to the parking lot where Mike pushed Twitch's mom down the sidewalk toward where Ryan and Ethan were waiting. "You and me need to have a conversation."

"No. You don't." Bea put a hand on her hip. "Leave it be. It's not any of his business, and it sure as hell isn't yours."

"What's going on?" Twitch glared at his sister. "Bea?"

"Nothing. Lummox here misunderstood a few things."

Twitch glared at Hazard. Someone had better give him some damn details. Soon.

"He had his hand on your throat," Hazard growled.

"What the fuck? Who? Mike?" The bastard was dead. No one laid his hands on Bea. She'd been through enough. "I swear to Christ, woman. Your taste in men is shit."

"We were horsing around. I'd taken the last candy bar and he was teasing! He said he'd kill me then it'd be his. Ryan even joined in. You saw that!"

"Babe, a good man doesn't tease about that shit. He sure as fuck doesn't with a woman with your history." Hazard gritted the words through clenched teeth.

"My history!" Bea's enraged glare went to Twitch. "Tell me you didn't tell him."

"I didn't tell him." Ethan had told everyone at Counterstrike. Bea and Ryan were under their protection. Always.

"Newsflash, you carry your baggage like armor. It doesn't take much to see you're mired in bullshit someone piled onto you. Since Twitch here is one of the best men I've met, it sure as shit wasn't him." Hazard glanced back at Mike. "You can do way better than that loser, babe."

"I'll keep that in mind for when I give a damn what you think." The woman turned and flounced away.

"I'm thinking bringing them here wasn't the best idea," Twitch said. "Asking you to do it may have been worse."

"It's not like that, man. I know better."

"I'd rather contend with you going after her than another asshole," he admitted.

Hazard's lips upturned into a smirk. He glanced over his shoulder. "Good enough."

A growl rose from Twitch. The man laughed, then turned and headed toward the food.

Twitch hung back and watched the byplay between Bea and Hazard. The woman fixed both of them plates, then got one for Ryan. The boy chattered nonstop with Ethan, then Milo. His typical shyness evaporated whenever Twitch's bosses and coworkers were around.

Because he felt safe surrounded by so many operatives.

The realization stung. The kid should feel safe no matter who was around him. Bea insisted the boy was fine, that he didn't need any further counseling than what he'd gotten the first year after she left Ryan's father. But Twitch disagreed. No kid should swing so far from total lockdown to full-on extrovert depending on who was around.

Right?

CHAPTER 11

Twitch's family was here. She halted her walk toward the man. Should she approach? Leave them be? She hovered for less than a minute when he turned and smiled.

"Angie, you okay? Why did you stop?" He held his arm out. "Come meet my family."

Okay then. Nervousness crawled through her. Did they know she was being helped by Counterstrike? What if they got the wrong idea and thought she and Twitch were together? She tugged on the baggy T-shirt she'd worn. The ratty jeans weren't exactly impressive either. The fact both were covered with dirt and grime from the cleanup effort didn't help.

"Hi." A beautiful, female version of Twitch held out her hand. "I'm Beatriz, but everyone calls me Bea. I'm John's little sister. That's his real name, by the way. He and the others have such ridiculous names."

The woman's eye roll made Twitch chuckle. Angie's stomach tightened and her heart clenched when she saw the way the man looked at his sister.

Love.

Family.

God, it'd been too long since she'd been around her family. Brief videos weren't the same. Angie shook the woman's hand and forced conversation despite the nervousness. "It's a pleasure to meet you."

"Hi, I'm Ryan." The little boy hovered between Twitch and an older woman in a wheelchair.

Twitch put a hand on the boy's shoulder. "This is my friend Angie."

Ryan's eyes widened. "Cool! You're the one who's like a ninja! Uncle Ethan and Uncle Milo both said so. I wanna learn!"

Angie couldn't help but laugh when the boy jumped into a classic karate pose, then kicked out with enough force to almost tumble over. Twitch splayed a palm on Ryan's back to keep him upright.

"He's doped up on an ice cream rush right now," Twitch said with a smile.

"Sorry about that," a man commented as he settled to a halt beside Bea. He held his hand out. "I'm Hazard, one of Counterstrike's new operatives."

"Joe. His name is *Joe*."

The man visibly tightened beside the woman. He wore his discomfort as a second skin and in the way his gaze constantly roamed the area. He'd been in the service and hadn't been out for long if Angie wasn't mistaken.

"You shouldn't do that," Angie said. Heat crept up her cheeks when both Twitch and Hazard looked at her, intensity in their eyes. "Sorry, but what they do is very important and dangerous."

"I know that," Bea snapped. "No offense, but the nicknames are stupid."

"To you, maybe. But not to them. I spent my entire life around men and women like Twitch and Hazard. Most of their nicknames are earned in battle. With blood. Some are funny reminders etched into existence by their comrades. Some of those comrades likely died beside them. So, no offense because I don't know you, but they aren't stupid. And, honestly, that's not even getting into the more serious work they're doing now. They're helping strangers out of very scary and dangerous situations without knowing whether the people they're risking themselves for aren't crazy."

Bea paled. The older woman beside her gasped and reached up to snatch Twitch's hand.

"What do you mean about them risking themselves?" Bea asked. "They're putting people up in houses, getting them jobs. It's good work, but not dangerous."

Was she for real? Angie shook her head and bit her lip. She'd already said too much. Both Hazard and Twitch watched the byplay. Neither moved to intervene, likely because they were at a loss for words.

"This isn't my business," Angie said.

"It is." Twitch put a hand on her back. "Bea's never fully understood what Counterstrike does. And she'd definitely never understood the nicknames."

"I didn't realize they meant anything," the woman whispered. She glanced up at Hazard. "Honestly."

"Whether they do or not isn't relevant. I could be a deranged psycho for all either of them knows. I could latch on to them because they've made me feel safe for the first time in months. Walking away from people who offer you that while getting nothing but headaches in return is hard. Nicknames keep them safe, keep the ones they love protected from someone who might not be able to let go. Real names are power. They can be searched. Hunted. Stalked."

"I think she gets it now," Hazard said softly. He touched Bea's back.

"That's why what they do is dangerous?" Bea asked.

"That and the fact they put themselves between their clients and whoever's after them," Angie said.

"They make it look so simple." Red tinged Bea's face. Eyes wide, she looked up at Twitch, then at Hazard. "I'm sorry. I didn't mean anything by it."

"We know." Twitch hugged his sister.

"She's right, Mom," Ryan said, his little fists clenched. "Uncle Ethan and Uncle Milo helped us when Uncle John couldn't. Then they all did it again. You don't get it. You never have."

Uh oh.

"Ry." Twitch grasped the boy's shoulder until he looked up. "We'll talk about this later. Okay?"

"Angie's in scary trouble like we were, right?" The boy's eyes shimmered. "Mom doesn't get it because she's always, always had you. Which meant she's always had Uncle Ethan and Uncle Milo and now Hazard and everyone else. Other moms and kids aren't that lucky. It's scary being alone and hiding. She knows, but she hasn't ever gotten it because she hasn't had to."

The boy's voice rose at the end as tears slid down his face. What the hell had she started? Guilt kept her quiet a moment. Twitch picked the boy up. Bea moved toward them, but Hazard held her back. Twitch walked toward the picnic tables with his nephew.

"I'm sorry," Angie whispered.

"Don't be," the older woman said. She moved her wheelchair up a bit. "I'm Twitch's mom, Delia. I should thank you. I think you finally got through to my daughter here. Lord knows none of us have."

"Mom." Bea snapped the word, but paleness still overtook her face. Her eyes shimmered with unshed tears. "Ryan's right. I've always had John. Twitch. I mean Twitch. And everyone else."

Twitch returned with Ryan a few moments later. The boy was hopping around and chattering excitedly like he hadn't just had a meltdown.

"Is he okay?" Angie asked. "I'm sorry I upset him."

"You didn't," Bea said. "My son's had troubles adjusting and that's my fault because I've ignored a few things. I'm starting to see that now."

"Enough of that. Let's go get some pie. I saw several pecan pies I wouldn't mind trying." Twitch's mom looked up at Angie. "That's my son's favorite."

Angie smiled. "It's one of my favorites too, but I think cheesecake is way better."

The declaration for pie shifted everyone's focus to a new task—dessert. Angie followed Twitch's family as they went through the short line and snatched up their favorites. Twitch grabbed a piece of pecan, then glanced over at Angie.

"They don't have cheesecake."

"I'll try the thing with peaches." Angie pointed at something at the corner with peaches.

"The thing with peaches?" Amusement filled his voice. "Angel, tell me you're joking."

"What? I like peaches."

"Figured that. You know that's peach cobbler, right?"

"Oh."

"You've never had peach cobbler?" Twitch picked up a bowl of it. "I'm not sure this should be your first taste. I might have to sample it first."

Angie laughed as he guided them toward a picnic table. He sat next to Ryan. Angie sat across from him. Twitch set the peach cobbler in front of her, but took a big spoonful and ate it. Laughter tumbled from her.

"Son, you have a dessert of your own," his mom admonished.

"She's never had peach cobbler," Twitch said. "I'm not letting her first taste be bad."

"You should make her a butter roll," Bea said. She looked over at Angie. "My brother's quite the baker."

"Oh, really?" Angie smiled when red rose in Twitch's cheeks. "I think that's cool. What's a butter roll?"

"The best damned thing you'll ever taste," Ethan said from the other side of the picnic table. He glanced down at the cake he'd gotten. "Suddenly this doesn't look as good. Now I want a butter roll."

"See what you started?" Bea asked her mom.

"Everyone should have it at least once," his mom said. She took her spoon and dipped it into the cobbler. She chewed. Swallowed. Shook her head. "No. That's not good enough for her to taste."

Twitch chuckled and dragged it away from Angie. "Sorry, she's right."

"Not fair. Give it over."

"Afraid I can't," Twitch said. He glanced down the table at Ethan. "If you or Milo will swing by the store and pick up the supplies, I'll make a butter roll for Angie."

Ethan glanced at his brother. "I can grab the supplies, drop them off. Milo can take your family home."

"I want a butter roll!" Ryan shouted.

"Next time," Bea said. "Remember what Hazard told us in the car on the way here. Your uncle is working right now. He's keeping Angie safe. We're only here because there's so many people to look out for her."

"Okay." The little boy's shoulders drooped.

"I'll make one for you when I get back home," Twitch promised.

"Everyone finish up. We'll head out in a bit," Ethan ordered.

Everyone left the picnic tables and headed to the trashcans. The partially eaten desserts dumped, Twitch guided them all to the vehicles.

"Hey, Angie!"

Angie startled hearing her name. She turned and waved back at Mickie. The woman motioned for her. Twitch placed a hand on Angie's waist when Quint moved toward them. Manuel and Theresa were with him.

She headed toward the two teenagers, but Twitch drew her back against his hard body. "You're not rushing anywhere with so many people around. Slow and steady. Head on a swivel."

Angie nodded. Her pulse quickened when she realized

she'd moved a larger distance from Twitch's family than she'd realized. "Sorry. For a moment I forgot about..."

"You're okay. You're safe here, but we aren't taking any chances." Hot breath fanned in her ear. "Thank you for what you said to Bea. She doesn't mean anything by it when she uses our real names, but it's an issue with Hazard and a couple of the others."

"Hazard just got out."

"You can tell."

"He's more guarded. Loud noises drew his attention quicker."

"It's only been a couple of months. He joined Counterstrike to be closer to his sister, Marisol."

Angie suspected Marisol wasn't the only one he wanted to be close to. He'd seemed quite close to Twitch's sister and nephew. She kept the thought to herself, though. She'd stirred up enough when it came to the man's family.

"Angie," Quint said when he came to a halt in front of her. Manual and Theresa stood on opposite sides of him. "They both wanted to chat with you."

"Are you okay?" Angie grasped Theresa's arms, then ran her hand down the girl's long hair. "I heard a little bit about what happened."

Tears shimmered in the girl's eyes. "I'm okay, thanks to Manuel. And you."

The girl vaulted into Angie's arms and sobbed. Manuel's jaw twitched as he crossed his arms and glared at anyone watching her fall apart. Pride filled Angie when she met the young man's gaze.

"Thank you for helping her," Angie whispered.

"Wouldn't have happened if you hadn't been there yesterday, in our face about standing up for one another and watching out for others," Manuel said. "Hearing her ask those questions, I knew."

"Manuel," the girl warned as she drew away from Angie and wiped her eyes.

"I knew she was in trouble. A few of us had known awhile, but she kept to herself and never admitted it when someone asked." The boy shook his head. "Hearing those questions, I knew what I'd heard was true."

"Manuel don't. It's not his fault."

"Bullshit. Your dad is a dick."

"Manuel!"

"Both of you settle down," Quint said, his voice firm. He offered an apologetic smile to Angie. "I knew you were worried about them both. When they asked about you, I figured I'd bring them over."

"And Wally? I haven't seen him around." Angie hadn't spent much time with the elderly man who ran the youth center, but she doubted he would've missed the cleanup effort.

"He was here earlier, but a couple of my friends took him back home right before you came," Mickie said as she approached. "He was really upset when he saw the center."

Manuel's jaw twitched as his gaze slid to the remnants of the youth center. "That never should've happened. I'll get witnesses for you, man. However many you need."

"We'll chat about that later," Quint said. "I don't want you putting yourself at risk."

"Those pendejos won't mess with me." The boy's gaze cut to Theresa. "Or her. I'll make sure of it."

Angie hoped the quiet police officer standing between the two teenagers had extra patrol units in the area for the next couple of weeks. Tensions would escalate once more arrests were made.

"Are you safe now, honey?" Angie asked Theresa.

The girl nodded. "My grandma is taking care of me. She's my mom's… she won't let Dad or his guys get near me."

"She lives across the street from us," Manuel said, his arms crossed.

"Good." Angie smiled. "I know it's hard, but you've got to let others take the lead on this rebuild and getting the neighborhood safe. You've done your part getting it started. I'm proud of you both. Especially you, Manuel."

Theresa glanced down at her feet. Manuel's chest puffed out slightly.

"You're both very smart and capable, which is why I know you'll listen to Wally and whoever else is in charge of building the new youth center. If you hear or see something that means trouble, you let Quint or another police officer know." Angie paused and looked at both the kids. "Part of being strong and smart is knowing when someone else is better suited to solve a problem."

"Is that what you're doing?" Manuel jerked his chin toward Twitch. "What's your story?"

"Someone I knew got hurt. I got angry and started kicking over trouble I couldn't handle alone," she admitted. "I tried and almost died a few times. Don't make the mistake I made and wait to tag someone else in."

"Are you safe now?" Theresa asked.

"I am." She touched the girl's arm. "You take care of

yourself, honey. Don't be afraid to talk to someone about what happened. I know it's scary and kind of embarrassing to talk to a stranger about what you're feeling, but it helps."

The girl nodded. "The lady I met last night was nice. She said we could talk whenever I'm ready."

"Good." Angie hugged the girl, then moved to Manuel. "You're a good man, Manuel. Trust your gut. It won't steer you wrong."

"Are you going to teach more classes?" Theresa asked.

Angie looked at Twitch. Regret filled her. She'd love to work with the kids longer, make sure they were all more confident in their ability to defend themselves and each other if necessary. But she was returning home to Philadelphia in the morning.

"We'll see what can be worked out once the youth center is open again," she said.

If things went well, she likely wouldn't return to San Antonio. Then again, there was no reason she couldn't fly down and do a few classes every so often.

Although she'd only spent a short amount of time with them, Angie would miss Mickie, Mack, Corrie, and the other women she'd met last night. They'd welcomed her into their fold like she belonged. Like she was important.

Twitch.

She wanted to explore the attraction she had to him, but their time together had a limit. Forcing the thought aside, she said goodbye to the two teenagers and thanked Quint for all his help. He and Cruz had made San Antonio a much different experience than the other cities she'd been in.

Thanks to them, her trust in law enforcement had been restored.

"I'm guessing we should go soon," she said to Twitch.

"Yeah." Twitch glanced over at the media crews. "The crowds are starting to thin out, which will shift more attention to us. We don't exactly blend in."

Angie chuckled. Nothing about Twitch and the other Counterstrike crew blended in. Neither did The Arsenal personnel. "You're going to Philadelphia, right?"

"I'm not leaving your side until this is over, Angie." He took her hand and turned her to face him. "Medina and his team will go with us, but we won't see them. Ethan is sending Hazard to help me keep you safe."

They wouldn't be alone. Angie stifled the frustration rising inside her. Her safety was more important. So was Twitch's. "Is he coming back to the safe house with us?"

"Yeah. Milo and Ethan will take my family home." He caressed her cheek. "You have an expressive face, Angel."

She peered up at him. "Sorry, I know I shouldn't, but I wish we could have tonight. Just you and me."

"I'm not sure that's a good idea. As much as I'd love a night with you, I doubt it'd be enough." He stroked along her mouth. "You're a beautiful woman, Angie. I'm drawn to you, but you've been through hell the past few months. I can't take advantage of that."

"You aren't. I'm smart enough to know what I want."

"I know you are, but that doesn't mean it should happen now," he whispered. "We both said we'd explore this once this is over. We will."

"With you in Austin and me in Philadelphia." She shook her head. "We both know how that'll end."

"No, we don't." He rested his forehead against hers. "I don't give up on something I want. I haven't wanted something this bad in a long time, Angel."

Angel. She loved the nickname when Twitch used it. She smiled. "I'm holding you to that."

"Good." He pulled away. "Come on, let's get you back to the house. I've got some butter rolls to make."

CHAPTER 12

Butter rolls were amazing. Angie took a deep breath and inhaled the remnant cinnamon and butter scents filling the house. It'd been a couple hours since Ethan dropped off the supplies and left. Twitch got to work making the sugary dessert.

Angie, Twitch, Hazard, and Medina had eaten large helpings of the sugar, butter, and cinnamon laden decadence with vanilla ice cream while watching a movie. When combined with the day's events, it'd almost been too much relaxation and normalcy.

She peered into the inky darkness on the other side of the bedroom window and wondered if going back to Philadelphia was the right thing. What if she scraped off the life she'd had there?

No. She couldn't let the bastard steal what she'd had.

She loved her dojo.

She loved the people she'd helped.

Emotion clogged her throat. For the first time in six months, she thought she might get it all back.

Because of Twitch and his friends.

And a group of strangers in Chicago who recognized she was in trouble and helped. Had she even remembered to thank Ben and Vani and Isa? She never even knew Isa's boyfriend's name. Were they okay?

And Matt. And his cop brother.

A soft knock at the door drew her attention. Twitch entered and scanned the room briefly, but his gaze settled on her quickly, as if he'd sensed her location immediately. Awareness arced within her as he prowled closer.

Anticipation hummed within her veins, a surge of need that tingled just beneath her skin.

"It's late. You should rest," Twitch said.

"I think I ate too much today," she admitted with a chuckle. "And I'm remembering there was a little bit of the butter roll left. I may have been waiting for you to sleep so I could sneak in and steal it."

"I hate to disappoint you, but Medina took it and two new ones with him when he left. He said the team deserved to enjoy them too," Twitch said. Intensity loomed within his dark gaze. "That's not why you're still awake. I can almost hear your sexy mind thinking."

He cupped her face and rested his forehead against hers. The tingles burst, tiny explosions of heat that spread through her as she basked in the physical contact. She splayed one hand on his chest and stroked his stubbled jaw with the other.

"Ben and Vani and Isa and the others in Chicago. Are they okay?"

"Yeah. Zoey sent a team just in case," Twitch said with a smile. "Ben's one of her most trusted assets within the area. Even if he wasn't involved, The Arsenal would've kept them all protected. That's what they do, especially for the network."

Emotion clogged her throat a moment as she tried to give voice to the thoughts she'd been alone with since finishing her shower over an hour ago. The surface-level concern for the people in Chicago had masked the true thoughts looming within her, waiting for the perfect moment to strike.

"Part of me doesn't want to go tomorrow," she whispered. "I'm finally safe. I actually had a normal day today. No one tried to kill me."

"It's normal to be scared," Twitch said. He stroked her arm. "Your last memories of Philly weren't good ones. It's natural to be worried about returning, but you aren't going alone."

She didn't want to think about tomorrow and what awaited her at home. She grasped the back of Twitch's neck and tugged forward until their hot breaths melded. Pleasure ignited when their mouths collided.

Angie deepened the kiss, swept her tongue into his mouth. A groan rumbled from him. The swift response quickened her pulse. Hands on her ass, he lifted her up. She wrapped her legs around his waist and arms around his neck as she maintained control of the kiss.

Twitch walked them backward until they fell onto the bed. Weight settled on her, between her legs as he took control of the kiss. The carnal tongue duel overrode any semblance of control. She writhed against him and wrapped her legs around him once again.

She clawed at his shirt until heat greeted her hands

along his back. Twitch snagged both her wrists and pinned them above her head. She pushed, but found herself locked beneath him as he seized control.

Need shot through her hardened nipples and arrowed downward. A moan escaped her mouth as he severed the kiss. She peered into his obsidian gaze. Molten arousal.

"I should walk away," he mumbled.

"Don't."

"I'd have an easier time landing on Mars than leaving you right now." He kissed along her cheek, nibbled her earlobe. "Tell me to leave."

"Stay." She writhed against him. "I want you, John."

"Fuck, just hearing your sexy voice say my name made my dick hard, Angie."

He stilled atop her. Hot breath fanned her ear as he surrendered the grip on her wrists. She ran her hands down his back, then beneath his shirt. Tugged upward.

"Tonight. For tonight, you're mine." She nipped his ear. "No rules. No regrets."

He ran his fingers through her hair as he kissed her once again. The slow glide of his lips across hers disappeared when he pulled away to help remove his shirt.

Yes.

Hot, toned skin greeted her hands as she caressed his back. His arms.

"You're killing my control, Angel," he whispered against her mouth.

"Good." She nipped his lower lip, then lifted up. Twitch took the cue and removed the baggy T-shirt she'd worn.

Awareness beaded along her skin in tiny goose bumps

as his gaze swept downward. Clad in panties only, she kept her attention on his face. Raw need etched itself across his handsome face, settled in the dark depths of his eyes.

His calloused fingertips ran along her neck then skimmed along the outer swell of her left breast. He stroked lower, pausing on the bandage. Sensing the turmoil within him, she repeated the contact on him, stopping on a scar.

"They aren't wounds," she whispered. "They're reminders of what we survived to be here."

She admired his muscular torso. She traced the grooved abdominal muscles and halted at each reminder he wore.

"Angie." The name was a plea mixed with a partial growl.

He scraped his thumb across her hardened nipple, then leaned down and licked the achy nub. Pleasure assailed her, flared through her. She clasped his head and moaned as heat enveloped her nipple. He sucked and flicked, taunting her until her entire body reacted.

She'd never been shy with sex, but Angie sensed intimacy with Twitch would be different. They separated long enough to remove the rest of their clothes. He stood beside the bed, a nude Adonis. No, far sexier. Anticipation quickened her pulse as she sat on the bed, her feet on the ground.

Twitch's thick, hardened cock drew her attention. A groan escaped him when she grasped his arousal. Intensity loomed within his eyes when their gazes met.

"Keep touching me like that and I won't last long." He grasped her hair as she pumped him a few times.

"We have all night," she whispered. She licked the pre-cum off the tip. Then cried out in shock when she went airborne. The mattress jostled with her weight as laughter tumbled from her. "That wasn't very nice. I was busy."

"Later," he growled. "After I've feasted on you."

Pleasure arrowed through her and pooled between her legs as he maneuvered onto the bed and pulled her thighs apart. He raised her head and settled a pillow there.

Amusement escaped her in a laugh. "It won't take me very long to come, John. One touch and I'll likely go off."

"Good, then I can watch you come apart for me several times before I feel you explode on my dick." He caressed her face, then kissed her.

She writhed upward to initiate contact lower, but he chuckled against her mouth. The kisses and nibbles alternated between gentle and rough. He stroked and pinched her nipples and massaged his way down her body in a sensuous, languid worship she'd never experienced.

"John."

His name tumbled from her lips as he kissed her lower stomach. He grasped her hips and lifted her just enough to reposition himself between her splayed legs. Their gazes locked as he kissed her mound and stroked her slit.

He parted her and plunged a finger into her as he thumbed her clit. A cry escaped her. Twitch froze a moment, then chuckled.

"You're a screamer. That could be a problem," he mumbled. "Hazard's in the living room."

"Damn." She thrust herself into his hand. "Don't you dare stop now."

"I'm not stopping, Angel. I've been thinking about tasting you too long."

He lapped her pussy, alternating his fingers and his tongue as he played. The soft moans he emitted shot need through her entire body as white-hot pleasure rippled through her. She grasped his head, shoulders, and any other part of him she could reach as the sensations built.

Twitch held her body firmly in place beneath him as he continued the ministrations. The orgasm assailed her faster than she expected. Awareness tunneled until only she and John existed. Her mind blanked as she rode the shockwaves of pleasure.

Her entire body sank into the mattress a moment. Then John moved, positioned himself above her. Their mouths fused in a molten kiss so carnal and filled with need her entire body reacted. He continued stroking her pussy and clit until the final wave overtook her.

"John." The name was a plea as she writhed beneath him. "Fuck me. Please. I want you inside me."

"I'm going to die if I don't feel you come around my dick," he whispered in her ear. "Relax, Angie. I've got you."

He kissed her and stroked her body a moment, then left. Cool air brushed across her heated skin. Shock riddled her brain a moment. He'd left?

No. Angie followed his path as he found his pants, pulled out his wallet and grabbed a foil packet. Right. Ever the protector. "I'm clean. I haven't been within anyone in so long I've lost track. I have an implant."

She offered the info in a rush of breathy words as their gazes locked. He returned to the bed and ripped the package open. Determined to savor his body as long as she could, she shifted her leg until her foot was on his hip. She maneuvered the other leg to his shoulder and flipped them.

Shock rolled across his face a moment before a grin spread. "Damn, that was hot."

Angie straddled his powerful thighs and took the condom. Pulling it from its package, she grasped the base of his long, thick cock with one hand as she rolled the protection on with the other. "You'd better have more than one of these because once won't be enough."

She positioned herself above him and guided him into her wet pussy. A moan escaped her when he grasped her hips and stilled. The fullness consumed her, awakened her need. She moved, slow at first. Hands splayed on his abs, she rode him in the rhythm she wanted. Although he grasped her hips, he gave her free rein over their lovemaking.

The thrusts deepened until her breaths fell in needy pants. The faster pace matched the desire building in her once more. She gasped when he pulled out and rolled them. A moan escaped her when she positioned herself on all fours. He grasped her legs and lifted.

"My turn," he growled as he thrust into her, so deep and hard her entire body trembled. He gripped her lower body, kept her lifted off the bed.

God. She screamed her release into the pillow as he plunged deeper and faster. The mattress springs creaked, the headboard banged against the wall.

"Angie." He cried her name out moments later and then collapsed atop her.

The added weight pressed her into the mattress. Utterly spent, she sighed in contentment and relished the feeling of him against her.

"Fuck, that just blew my mind," he whispered into her ear as he shifted them onto their side.

Angie relished the aftermath a few moments as their breaths fell in tandem. There were no awkward moments or thoughts. No regrets. She drew his arms tighter around her and sighed deeply.

"You're amazing," she whispered. "I'd offer more thoughts, but my brain moved to Tibet. It's going to become a monk and spend its life worshipping in the euphoria that is your lovemaking."

He chuckled and moved her hair from her neck. "Mine must've packed up and gone along for the trip. I've never lost myself with someone like that."

"Me neither," she whispered. The admission settled between them.

Wrapped in Twitch's arms she could almost pretend her troubles didn't exist. A part of her wanted to chat about the future, see if the two of them could navigate a long-distance relationship. Modern day technology made it much simpler from what she'd heard others say.

"We're going to make this work," he declared. "We'll find a way."

"We will." She groaned when he cupped her breast. "I know we should sleep, but I'm not done with you."

"Good, because there's no way we're through yet." He kissed her neck, then moved off the bed.

She squealed her surprise when he lifted her up and carried her into the bathroom. The cold counter beneath her ass a moment later made her shift uncomfortably.

Twitch disposed of the condom, then moved to the shower and started the water. He looked through the drawers and chuckled when he pulled out a box of condoms. "I don't even want to know why these are stocked automatically in safe houses. Then again, they're used for more than the network."

"They are?"

"Yeah. Arsenal wanted places for their operatives to crash or hide out if needed," Twitch said.

Anticipation awakened her pulse when he prowled toward her. She spread her legs and wrapped her arms around him when he stood between them.

Images of a soapy, wet Twitch flashed through her thoughts as they kissed. She'd never had sex in a shower before. Legs wrapped around his waist, she deepened the kiss. Firm hands grasped her ass and lifted her from the counter.

Angie shoved all concerns about what awaited her aside. All that mattered was savoring every second she had with Twitch.

* * *

TWITCH LOOKED DOWN AT ANGIE AND SWEPT HER RIOTOUS hair from her beautiful face. He slid on a pair of shorts and headed into the living room. Hazard sat in the seat nearest the television, which was switched to a sports channel.

"I'm surprised you're up, much less out here," the man commented.

Twitch didn't respond. Truth told, he wanted nothing more than to freeze time and have tonight last longer. He grabbed a couple of bottled waters from the fridge. He uncapped one and took a deep pull of it as he headed back into the living room and sat on the sofa.

Turmoil kept him silent. A part of him regretted making love to Angie. Walking away from her wasn't possible, not now. Yet he couldn't mentally navigate a way past the road-blocks they'd face if they wanted a happily ever after.

She had a life in Philly, one she'd worked damn hard to forge. He had a career he loved and a family he had to care for in Austin.

"You shouldn't have to choose," Hazard commented. "None of my business, but if I was you, I'd pick her. Hands down."

Twitch took another drink of water and glared at the man. He hadn't come out for advice. Had he? Fuck.

He set the half empty bottle beside the full one and ran his hand through his hair. "I didn't mean for this to happen."

"You're good together. The chemistry is magnetic. Anyone with half a brain can see you two connected on a level few do."

"It's too quick, man. She's been through hell the past several months."

"And? She's a beautiful, smart, and amazing woman. You're one hell of a guy who's lived a life where decisions are made in seconds, not months." Hazard shook his head.

"Men like us know what we want immediately. We don't dick around when something's important to us. At least, we shouldn't."

"She won't leave Philly, and I can't leave Austin."

"Bullshit." Hazard chuckled. "Man, I get that you love your family. Fuck knows I tapped out of service to be closer to Marisol, but I wouldn't upend my life or put it up on a shelf for her."

Twitch's gut clenched. "I'm not shelving my life."

"You're out here thinking about your sister and her kid and your mom rather than back there with a woman who's clearly blown your mind." Hazard leaned forward and rested his elbows on his knees. "Don't tap out without giving it a shot. Angie's worth whatever hassles you might encounter."

"I know that," Twitch gritted out.

"Then why the fuck are you out here?"

"Maybe I just needed water."

"Right." Hazard chuckled. "We've lived entire lives doing the shit we did for our country. We've stared death in the eyes a thousand times and defied the odds to make it back to civilian life. Whatever the fuck that is. I've gotta believe there's a reason we did all that."

Twitch looked away as the man's words sank into him. "Seeing Ethan with Marisol... he changed. Whatever darkness he brought back with him disappears a little more each day because of her."

"That's what we fought for. That's why we did whatever we had to, for the right to come back and get that for ourselves."

"Bea needs me. Ryan too. And Mom…" Twitch shook his head. "I need to be in Austin for them."

"No, you don't. Hate to say it, man, but that sister of yours needs a kick into reality. She's had you, Ethan, Milo, and everyone else coddling her for too long. You all did a good job getting her safe from that bastard, but it's time to step back and let her find solid ground on her own."

Twitch suspected Hazard fully intended to be around to help Bea find that solid ground, but he didn't comment. For once, he couldn't argue the logic because he'd thought the same thing many times the past year.

None of that mattered tonight, though. The mission to get Angie safe was still underway and would likely take a while. Problems as serious as hers wouldn't end overnight. Then again, Counterstrike and The Arsenal made troubles far worse than hers go away quickly. It's what they did.

"You aren't in this alone, man. We've got your six. Whatever you want, we'll make it happen."

Twitch grunted. "Not sure I've said this, but I'm glad you tapped out. You're a great addition to the team."

"Glad to hear it. Now get your ass back to that bed before she wakes up."

CHAPTER 13

"Ms. Bierman, a great deal of this could have been avoided if you'd kept us apprised of the threats and attacks." Detective Shuler leaned his lanky body back in the chair and sighed heavily.

"My client did, on multiple occasions." Jennifer glared across the narrow table at the Philadelphia detective and plopped a file folder on the table. "We are here to assist your investigation. An organization we've contracted has obtained video surveillance of the attacks, both in Philadelphia and the majority of those in other cities. They have also linked payments for those attacks to a shadow corporation. It's our belief that organization belongs to Noah Wints."

"Mr. Wints has been cleared of any involvement in Ms. Bierman's attacks—a fact that we would have shared if she'd remained in the city." The detective leaned forward and picked up the thick file. "Please don't take this the wrong way, but we aren't going to take the word of an out-of-state private detective about anything. While I appreciate Ms. Bierman was frightened for her life, she never should have fled."

"We will agree to disagree on that one," Jennifer said. "As for The Arsenal being an out-of-state private detective, I assure you they are not the bargain bin organization you are implying they are. Nor is Counterstrike. Underestimating either of our groups will likely land you in trouble you can't get your way out of, Detective."

"Thank you for bringing Ms. Bierman in to clear things up. I will review her statement and corroborate it with any surveillance footage I can obtain in the area at the time of the alleged attack." The detective glared at Angie. "We don't condone vigilantes."

"Had your department done its job and kept my client safe, she never would have been forced to defend herself. Furthermore, she wouldn't have fled if, again, she would have felt safe." Jennifer stood. "I believe we are done here, Detective. Please see that the charges against my client are cleared by the end of the week. I'd hate to see this situation escalate."

"We aren't done. I have more questions about the out-of-state attacks."

"You have the information we've gathered. Footage we obtained has been emailed to you." Jennifer picked up her briefcase. "You'll need to get any information beyond that from the investigating agent."

"Investigating agent?" Detective Shuler stood. "I'm the investigating detective."

"For the attack here, yes. The multiple attacks and stalking across state lines are not yours. Those, along with the attempted hack into a federally-protected system are matters for the FBI to investigate." Jennifer held out her hand. "I look forward to hearing from you soon, Detective. Thank you."

The detective shook the woman's hand. Angie stifled the chuckle rising in her throat. Aside from the short to-the-point answers she'd provided earlier, Angie hadn't spoken much at all. Jennifer Davenport was one hell of an attorney—one who apparently had passed the bar in several states, one of which was Pennsylvania since she'd initially started with a small law firm in Pittsburg.

Angie remained silent as they made their way out of the room. Twitch, Ethan, and Hazard were fanned out within the interior of the lobby area. They fell into step behind her and Jennifer as they left the building.

"Status?" Ethan asked.

"They're as stubborn and ignorant as we expected," Jennifer said. "They'll likely drag their feet, but the local assault charges against Angie will be dropped. The evidence substantiating her self-defense is too overwhelming."

"You were amazing," Angie said. "I barely even talked. Jennifer was on the attack the entire time."

"He had the unmitigated gall to call The Arsenal an out-of-state private detective." Red rose in Jennifer's face.

Twitch chuckled. "Remind me not to ever piss you off."

"We should've put more time between our meeting here and the one with the FBI," Jennifer commented as they got into the rental vehicle. Angie crawled into the middle.

Heat spread through her when Twitch settled at her

other side. His hand rested on her upper thigh. "You okay?"

The question was a barely audible whisper against the shell of her ear. Angie nodded. "Thanks to all of you, I am. That went better than I expected."

"Let's hope the rest of the day does," Twitch muttered.

"Are you expecting trouble? Did something happen?" Jennifer looked at the two men.

"We discussed this, Jen. Wints likely had eyes on us the moment we landed," Ethan said.

"How?" Angie asked.

"The flight manifest had your name on it," Twitch said. "A man with his reach, he has eyes everywhere."

Sourness coated her stomach. She didn't want the temporary reprieve she'd had to end, but she knew coming home was the right step. She didn't fear a confrontation with Noah Wints. Truth told, she'd give just about anything for ten minutes alone with the bastard.

"Can we grab some coffee somewhere before we head to the FBI offices?" Jennifer asked. "I'm about two quarts too low to tango with another suited asshole."

Hazard chuckled. "First off, we aren't going to the FBI offices for the meeting. She asked to meet us at Angie's dojo. Second, from what Cruz and Zoey said, this meeting will likely go very different."

"How so?" Angie asked.

"Special Agent Victoria Blevins knows The Arsenal," Ethan said. "She's assisted with a number of human trafficking cases The Arsenal brought to the FBI's attention. She's also worked with Cruz on a few cases."

"And she's from the Philly office?" Twitch asked. "That's convenient."

"She's from D.C.," Ethan said. He pulled the vehicle onto the road. "She inserted herself because of the hack into HERA via the safe house."

"So it is federally-protected? I thought that was horse shit." Angie looked at Jennifer when the woman started laughing.

"I try not to throw horse shit around. But, yes, it is a highly classified system. I doubt Agent Blevins even has clearance to know much about it," Jennifer said. "She may be a perceived ally, but we play this the same way we did with Detective Shuler. Don't answer any question until I say it's okay."

"She's holding the meeting at the dojo to throw you off," Twitch said. "That's what I'd do if I was her."

"Get Angie in her own environment, give her a sense of security," Hazard added. "It's a smart play."

It was. Angie hadn't been in her dojo for six months. She glanced at the time on the console. Two in the afternoon. Would it even be open? During the week she typically left it open even though it was slow, mainly because she was there anyway.

Had Claude kept the same hours, or had he changed things? The brief glances of the dojo's website she'd chanced while on the run hadn't shown any changes, but that didn't mean anything.

Ethan didn't ask for directions or an address, which meant the man had likely done enough research to know exactly where he was going.

The man glanced over his shoulder at her. "What you

did in San Antonio was good. You had a huge impact in a very short timeframe. Chuck, the youth center's regular instructor, wanted to train with you, get your advice on how to proceed."

"Really?" Angie's voice rose an octave from surprise. "Why?"

"Because I met with him, showed him what all you'd accomplished with your dojo here in Philly. He was impressed." Ethan glanced at her again. "You're a natural leader."

"I like what I do."

"It shows," Twitch said.

"When this is all over, I'd like to sit down and chat," Ethan said. "Milo and I came up with an idea we'd like your help with."

"Oh?" Angie couldn't hide her curiosity.

Ethan chuckled. "It'll wait until this is all over."

She hoped it was something that would help her stay in touch with Counterstrike, and therefore Twitch. Last night had been amazing. No one had ever made her feel so cherished and treasured. She'd shared more about herself and become closer to him in one night than she ever had with most everyone else she'd dated.

Safe.

She'd felt safe to be herself. She hadn't had to hold back her somewhat dominant sexual needs. Twitch was comfortable enough with his sexuality to be playful and cede control when she wanted. Awareness arced within her when she looked over and saw the intensity in his gaze.

He was the first man to assume control with ease.

Most men she'd dated in the past weren't as adept with martial arts as she was. Sure, that didn't matter. It wasn't like sex was a competition, but being with a man more than capable of taking her on had added an unexpected depth to their encounter.

Trust. Safety.

She'd felt protected enough to let go. She'd trusted Twitch to keep her safe and accept her as she was at her most vulnerable. He hadn't turned their lovemaking into a sport, a competition, like her last ex had. Her past lovers had always treated her like martial arts expert Angie. With Twitch she was just Angie.

Excitement filled her when the vehicle pulled up across the street from her dojo. Ethan's cell phone chimed as they exited the vehicle. Twitch grasped Angie's hand. She peered across the street at the one-story white building she'd poured her heart and soul into. The mural Benny and Clay had started after she'd fled was complete and filled the entire right side of the front. The gorgeous representation of the local neighborhood stirred Angie's pulse.

She crossed the street and studied the beautiful artwork. Benny and Clay both had wicked talent with portraits. She traced the wrinkles around Mr. Hassan's smile. The man's weathered face drew her attention first, but there were so many others.

"It's beautiful," Jennifer whispered.

"I hired them the night I left Philly," Angie commented. "Benny and Clay kept getting in trouble for tagging local buildings. When I found out they'd flushed the drugs planted in my dojo to protect me from the cops, I asked them to do a mural. Whatever they wanted."

"They've got talent," Twitch said. He motioned toward the lower right corner. "Clearly you made an impression."

Angie squatted. Shock rolled through her as she read the words scrawled at the bottom of the mural.

Respect is earned, not taken. ~Angie, the soul of the hood.

She stood on wobbly legs. Emotion clogged her throat. She'd fled Philly to keep everyone around her safe, but she doubted anyone understood that. There'd been no time to tell anyone—except for the harried orders she'd given two teenaged boys.

"Come on, let's get inside," Twitch whispered.

Right. Inside. Music pulsated from the overhead speakers when they entered. She recognized the song immediately as one she always used during the final moments of the kickboxing class. Four steps later and she was at the far back of the smallest room.

Mats filled most of the space. A cluster of people faced the back wall where Claude stood, going through the final motions of the cool down phase of the class. Shock registered on the man's face, but he continued the movements until the song ended.

"I'll see you on Friday," he said. "Great job, everyone!"

Everyone picked up their mats. Several took them directly to the storage area. A few gasped and dropped their mats and ran toward her.

"Angie! Angie's back!"

Shrieks and shouts echoed within the small room. Claude shook his head, a big grin on his face. He stood back as the cluster surrounded her. Twitch remained at her side, but didn't shove or push anyone away as they took turns hugging and welcoming her back.

Tears shimmered in her gaze as she greeted everyone.

Where have you been? Are you okay? Are you back for good?

The questions ricocheted around her. Claude's dark gaze flashed with annoyance. Hands fisted, he looked away as everyone continued to pepper her with inquiries and chatter.

"I'm okay. I can't talk about it right now, but I'm okay," Angie said.

"Are you back for good?" Yvonne asked. "It hasn't been the same without you here."

"Everything's still a bit complicated right now. I promise I'll let you know as soon as I can." She broke apart from the cluster of people. "Thank you for the warm welcome. I'm sorry I left without letting everyone know. It looks like you all have been doing great. Thanks to Claude."

She maneuvered until she stood beside the man who'd taken over in her absence. She owed him a lot of apologies, gratitude, and answers. He remained silent as everyone continued peppering her with conversation and questions.

"Okay, everyone." Twitch's voice rose over the hum of chatter. "Angie just got in. Let's give her some room and time to acclimate. She'll brief you later. Not today, likely not tomorrow. But soon."

He settled an arm at her waist and guided her out of the cluster. She motioned toward the back corridor, which led to an office. Claude fell in step behind them.

Silence loomed when they entered what'd once been her office. She scanned the room, noted none of her personal possessions on the desk or walls. Claude's plaques and pictures filled the desk and walls. Tension tightened her stomach.

"Where the fuck have you been?" Claude shouted the question as he slammed the door and closed in on her.

Twitch tensed behind Angie but didn't move to stand in front of her. Pride filled her. He knew she could handle her own battles.

"Back off," Angie warned when Claude entered her personal space.

"You have a hell of a lot of nerve walking in here like you didn't ghost this place, me, and everyone else." The man turned, took a step away. He ran his hand through his short hair. "Fuck. Six months, Angie. Not. One. Fucking. Call."

"I'm sorry."

"You're sorry?" Claude thundered the question.

Twitch put an arm on Angie's waist and moved in front of her. "Angie might be okay with you screaming at her, but I'm not. Settle down or this conversation is over."

"Who the fuck are you?" Claude asked, his narrowed gaze on Twitch. "What is going on, Angie? Who is this guy? Where the hell have you been?"

The door opened. Hazard slid in and leaned against the wall. Arms crossed, he raised his eyebrows, but made no comment when Claude glared at him.

"Claude, I'm sorry, but you know it wasn't safe for me to stay here," Angie said. "I couldn't risk someone else getting hurt like Chastity."

"I would've protected you," he clipped. "You should've called."

"I couldn't chance contact with anyone. I ran into Benny and Clay the night I left. They were supposed to get word to you, warn you about the threats."

"They did. That should've come from you, Angie. One phone call before you left. Was that too much to ask?"

"Claude…"

"I tried filing a missing person report and was told you'd been in contact with your father." Claude fisted his hands. "You told him, but you couldn't be bothered to let me know."

Guilt kept her quiet a moment. She took a step forward, moved between Twitch and Claude. "You knew I had a plan. I told you. Remember?"

"Didn't think you'd ever run. That's not you." He put his hands on his hips. "I packed your shit up from your apartment after I convinced your landlord not to seize it all. I paid the two months' rent and utilities you owed out of the dojo's account, which I thank fuck had access to. Your shit's in a storage unit, not that you must give a damn since you left without any of it."

God. She hadn't even thought about the apartment. She should have. Claude had been added to the dojo's bank accounts a few months before Hannah's murder because he did most of the administrative stuff.

"I'm sorry."

"Shit, Angie. You left with nothing. I just knew something had happened to you. Most women would flip without their stuff. Who the hell leaves without anything?"

"I had what mattered. I was raised by a military parent, Claude. I never placed much importance on possessions."

"Or friends," Claude bit angrily. "You shouldn't have run off like that."

"I wasn't going to let the bastard hurt anyone else because of me." She fisted her hands. "Would you have preferred I stay and let someone else get hurt like Chastity?"

"I would've protected you. You had options." Claude's gaze flicked to Twitch. "Where did you find him?"

"It's a long story." One she wasn't going into, not with Claude.

Unease pricked her skin when the man's focus returned to her. She'd never taken his interest in her seriously. "I'm sorry, Claude. I should've contacted you."

His jaw twitched. "Are you okay?"

"As okay as I can be." She motioned to Twitch. "This is Twitch. Hazard is the guy behind him. The one outside is Ethan, with his sister Jennifer. They're helping me sort some of my troubles."

"You trust strangers, but you wouldn't let me help." Claude shook his head. "Fuck."

"Everyone has a skillset. This is theirs."

"How can I help?" The man looked at Twitch. "Whatever you need, I'll help."

"Appreciated. Has anyone been around asking questions that shouldn't?" Twitch crossed his arms.

"Other than the whole neighborhood?" The man shook his head. "No, but we had a few break-ins when she first left. My apartment was tossed. My cell phone got stolen."

Silence loomed. Angie's heart quickened. Claude's place had been tossed.

"That's why you didn't contact me," Claude said. "I get it, Angie. Still burns that I couldn't help when you needed it."

"You did." She hugged the man. "You kept this place running. I knew you would. I never doubted you could manage the dojo without me. That's what I needed from you. And thank you for dealing with my apartment. I didn't mean to leave so much for you to handle. I'm sorry."

The man cleared his throat when Angie pulled away. He motioned toward the desk. "I'll get my stuff out of here. I wasn't going to move into here, but a few of the regulars thought it'd set a better tone if I did."

"Keep the office." Angie smiled. "You've earned it, and we both know I never used it anyway."

"I'm so glad you're okay. I've been worried sick," Claude said. He reached for her, then pulled away at the last minute. "We can sit down and catch up later."

"Yeah, I'd like that." Angie motioned toward the door. "I'd better get back out there."

Because an FBI agent would be arriving soon. Angie followed Claude back out. Hopefully they could navigate their way back to a normal routine. She was halfway down the narrow corridor leading to the main part of the dojo when Twitch grasped her waist.

Claude froze.

"We'll be out in a minute," Twitch said.

Hazard slapped Claude on the back. "Why don't you

show me around? We'd like to put up some extra security cameras. You can point out the best spots."

"Drones? You're putting drones into my dojo?" Angie looked up at Twitch.

"Yeah, and around the neighborhood." Twitch cupped her face. "Are you okay?"

"He was more upset than I expected."

"He wants you."

"He knows that's not happening."

"You never mentioned that before," Twitch commented. "We'll need to do a deeper dive into him."

"He wouldn't hurt me." Angie shook her head. "Claude wouldn't ever…"

"I trust no one when it comes to your safety," Twitch said. He ran his thumb across her lips. "You handled him well in there."

"He's right, you know. I should've contacted him, made sure he knew I was going through with my plan to leave and hideout awhile." She swallowed.

"When would you have done that? After running from three attackers? Before you found out about the cops raiding your dojo?"

Angie squeezed her eyes shut.

"You did what you had to do that night," Twitch said. "He'll get that. If he doesn't, that's his problem. Not yours."

Twitch was right. "You want a personal tour of my dojo?"

He grinned. Anticipation vibrated within her when he wrapped an arm around her.

"I'd love the private tour."

CHAPTER 14

"I thought we were meeting a fed here," Twitch commented as he drew to a stop beside Ethan, whose gaze was locked on Angie and Claude on the other side of the gym. "We need a deeper dive into him."

"Already in process," Ethan said. "She's got one hell of a setup here."

Twitch tightened. "She does."

"It'd be hard for her to walk away from this."

"Not sure anyone with half a brain would ask her to." Twitch fisted his hands. "There a point to this conversation?"

"You know there is." Ethan crossed his arms. "She's an amazing woman. You two would be great together. If you want something with her, you should pursue it. We'd help you make it work."

Twitch had spent more time than he cared to admit mulling over options after the incredible night they'd spent together. He'd never felt so comfortable with anyone. It was as though they'd known each other for years rather than days.

But his family had to be the priority right now, which meant staying in Austin. He couldn't rely on his sister to care for their mom, and asking Ethan and Milo to do anything more than they already were wasn't fair.

The pending separation from Angie wasn't something he wanted to discuss. He focused on the fed. "Where's the fed?"

"She texted, told us to meet her at the coffee shop down the street," Ethan said. "You up for a walk?"

"Sure." He looked over at Angie. "Let me get her."

He closed the distance between them quickly. His heartbeat quickened when she noticed his approach when he was only halfway there. He froze when he noted her thinned lips and tense stance. "Everything okay?"

"Fine. Claude and I were just discussing plans for tonight."

"Tonight?" Twitch looked at the man.

"It's dinner. We have a lot to discuss and catch up on, Angie. We may as well eat while we do it."

What the fuck? Was the man seriously asking her out to dinner? Twitch ignored the jealousy surging within him because A) he had zero reason to be possessive and B) he trusted Angie to make decisions for herself because she didn't belong to anyone.

"And I've already told you repeatedly that I can't. Not tonight, or anytime soon. Twitch and Hazard have worked hard to keep me safe. I'm not going to jeopardize them or their efforts by being careless." Angie sighed and ran her hand down her face. "Tell you what, we can order in and go over everything after the class tonight—that's assuming there's still a class tonight."

"There is." The man clipped the words. "That'll do. Later. It looks like your caveman here wants to haul you away."

Claude left before Twitch reacted to the caveman comment. "I should club the bastard over the head and teach him some damn manners."

"I don't think he understands how risky it still is for me," she said. "I've been gone a long time. There is a lot to go over."

The man knew exactly how dangerous it was. He just didn't give a damn about anything except spending time alone with Angie. While Twitch understood the compulsion, Claude didn't get time alone with her unless she wanted it and it wouldn't put her at risk.

"Claude can wait until tonight." He motioned to where Ethan stood. "The FBI agent wants to meet us at the coffee shop down the street."

"I thought she was coming here."

"Change of plans."

Angie took his hand, interwove their fingers, and headed toward the exit. They were half a block away from the dojo when she froze. A blonde woman sprinted toward them.

"Angie!"

"Chastity?" Angie said the woman's name as the two women embraced. "My God. I'm so glad to see you. How are you doing?"

"Better now that I know you're safe. I'm so sorry for

the things I said before you left." Tears shimmered in the woman's gaze. "I hope you aren't mad at me."

"Never." Angie hugged the woman again. "I'm so sorry you got hurt."

"I'm okay. I've been going to a group therapy and it's helped. Claude's worked with me, showed me a few more defense moves and got me back into my routines with the dojo." The woman smiled. "It hasn't been the same without you."

"I'm glad you're recovering. We'll have to get together and chat soon," Angie said. She looked over at Twitch. "This is my friend, Twitch. He's been helping me sort out a few problems."

"Hi." The blonde smiled at him. "You're huge! Damn, Ang. Where did you find him? Please tell me he has a twin."

Twitch chuckled and put his arm around Angie's waist. "Nice to meet you, Chastity."

"Are you coming to the class tonight?"

"Yes! Are you leading it?" Chastity asked. "I can't wait to catch up with you. I'm in a new apartment, not too far from where yours was actually. I helped Claude pack your stuff up and put it in storage. He couldn't remember which apartment was yours and the landlord wouldn't say. He was kind of a dick about the whole thing when we got there."

"Thank you, and I'm sorry you had to deal with all of that."

"I didn't mind. I'm just glad I remembered which unit was yours," Chastity said with a smile. "When you're ready I can take you over to the storage unit. I'd be lost without my stuff. I'm not sure how you managed without some of it."

Not much was needed when you were running for your life. Twitch bit back the response lodged in his throat. He wanted Angie off the street.

"Oh, great. We'll catch up after class, okay?"

"Cool! See you later." The blonde walked away, heading toward the dojo.

Twitch waited until they were several steps away. "How does she know where you live?"

"She asked about a good apartment complex in the area back before..." Angie's voice drifted off.

"Right." Twitch didn't believe in stereotyping a person's recovery process, but he didn't trust the woman. She seemed... off. "How long did you know her before the attack?"

"A few months, maybe. She's a dancer and wanted to have better defense techniques. Some of her frequent customers were handsier than she liked." Angie halted. "Why are you asking so many questions about Chastity. She was attacked. She's a victim in all of this, Twitch."

"I know." He glanced back, noted the woman watching them from the sidewalk in front of the dojo. "I don't trust anyone you knew before this started, Angie."

"I get that, but she got hurt because of me."

"You didn't hurt her." He cupped Angie's face. "None of this is your fault."

"I know, but I can't help but feel partially responsible."

Twitch kissed her lips and sighed. "We'll get this sorted, Angie. Then we'll figure out the rest."

"The rest?"

"You and me. Philly and Austin." He rested his forehead against hers. "I'm not walking away from what we have."

"Good, neither am I. I'd hate to have to stalk you," she said with a grin. "Come on. We'd better get into the coffee shop. It fills up quick when the school down the block lets out."

The cafe was a local shop with murals similar to the one at the dojo on its exterior walls. Angie startled seeing them. Her eyes brightened and she beamed a smile up at Twitch.

"They did more than just mine. This is fantastic!"

"It is." Twitch opened the door to the cafe and guided her inside. Ethan sat at a six-seat table in the far back corner. A dark-haired woman sat across from him. Jennifer was beside her brother.

Twitch let Angie sit first and grunted his approval when she sat next to Jennifer rather than the stranger. He sat beside the fed, but kept his gaze on Angie, who narrowed hers when she studied the woman.

"I know you," Angie said.

"This is Special Agent Victoria Blevins, from the DC office," Ethan said.

"You were in Claude's class when we came in. You were in the middle, toward the side wall." Angie crossed her arms. "You were in my dojo."

"I've been in your dojo the past two days, actually. The Arsenal contacted me, then Cruz Livingston got ahold of me when he found out I'd made some inquiries about you and your situation." The woman glanced at Twitch, then Ethan. "I'm not fully apprised of your plan, or The Arsenal's, but I've seen a couple of their operatives in the neighborhood."

"You recognized them?"

"I recognized their type. Operatives tend to stand out, even when trying to blend in." Agent Blevins motioned toward the waitress. "Do you want me to flag her down so you can place an order?"

"I believe my client would rather get started, Agent Blevins," Jennifer said. "I'm sure you understand how stressful this entire situation has been."

"Of course."

Twitch leaned back in the small chair and winced when it creaked beneath his weight. The woman wasn't the typical snail-paced fed he'd expected.

Agent Blevins clicked on a recording device and recited her name, location, and who she was with, along with why. Then she glanced at Angie. "I'm ready whenever you are. Please walk me through what has happened the past six months. Try and not leave anything out. Every small detail could be important."

Pride rose in Twitch when Angie didn't begin her recount until Jennifer nodded that it was okay.

"Everything?" Angie asked.

"Yes," Agent Blevins said. "The more we know, the faster we will find whoever is responsible."

"You've done nothing wrong, Angie. If you start speaking about something I'm uncomfortable with, I'll let you know," Jennifer said.

Twitch folded his arms and steeled himself for a full recount of what'd happened to Angie. While he'd likely heard everything, he'd never heard everything at once. A waitress came to take their order. He asked for water and coffee for himself and Angie.

Anger rose in Twitch when the brave woman he'd come to care about recounted attack after attack, her movement from city to city. What she'd endured and survived amazed Angie. He knew battle-hardened soldiers who wouldn't have done as well as she had.

Agent Blevins remained silent during most of the testimony. She paused a few times, asked pointed questions about the Atlanta attack—which had been the first death as a result of Angie's self-defense maneuvers.

Jennifer took notes as she sipped her coffee. Her astute gaze remained on Agent Blevins the entire time. The agent wrote notes the entire time as well. When she wasn't scrawling on the pad before her, she watched Angie—whose gaze remained locked on the table. A haunted expression remained within her beautiful brown eyes. By the time Angie expended a heavy sigh and halted her rapid flow of words, tension filled the atmosphere.

"Surveillance footage provided by The Arsenal corroborates most of what you recounted," Agent Blevins said. "I'll have agents within the local field offices dispatched to get witness testimonies."

Twitch grunted. He doubted there'd be many witnesses to testify from what they'd seen on the surveillance footage.

"New information came to light last night," Blevins said. "Ms. Plast used to dance at the same club Chastity worked at until a month before the attack."

"I didn't know that," Angie whispered, her face pale. "They were in the same class and never spoke. Chastity never said she knew Hannah outside the dojo. Why wouldn't she have said something after she was..."

"That's one of the things I want to find out. We could drag Chastity into an interrogation room and ask questions, but I'd rather have more to go on before we show our hand." Blevins took a sip of her coffee. "Ms. Plast also had an intimate relationship with Claude."

"No, she didn't," Angie argued. "I would've known. That's against the dojo policies. Claude and I both agreed it wasn't a good idea to become too close to our customers."

"Clearly he didn't agree," Ethan said. "You think Claude is involved in these attacks somehow?"

"I think there's more to this than a surface-level view offers," Blevins said. "There are additional suspects I'll be reviewing."

"Suspects?" Angie asked. "Who?"

Jennifer touched Angie's hand and shook her head. "That's not our business, Angie."

Twitch hated the shock on Angie's face. His gut tightened when Blevins turned off the recorder. She wouldn't like hearing what Agent Blevins was likely about to say.

"Ms. Davenport is correct. In a typical investigation we wouldn't share much."

"This isn't a typical investigation," Ethan said. "Most of what you have likely came from The Arsenal. And us."

"It has. It'll need to be corroborated, which will be our first priority," Blevins said. "With that said, I'll say that we will be looking into Claude and Chastity."

The swift statement rippled tension through the air as Angie leaned back from the shock. He wanted to reach for her, but kept his distance and let her process what the woman had just said. Admiration filled him when she didn't immediately refute the woman's assertion.

"Why Claude? I can admit Chastity knowing Hannah is weird. I don't understand how she could have attacked herself, but I will believe she might know more about Hannah's murder than she admitted. That would explain why she was attacked." Angie shook her head. "But Claude is the one I can't believe. I'm sorry, but he wouldn't hurt me."

"I can't discuss an ongoing investigation with you, Ms. Blevins. I can, however, offer a summary of what Counterstrike already knows since they're working with The Arsenal. Noah Wints inserting himself into your life immediately after Hannah's murder is suspicious. Chastity's and Claude's association with her prior to her death also needs to be investigated."

"Hannah saw a vehicle following her. Noah owns a vehicle like that. I saw it on the list." Embarrassment filled her.

"Let's chat about the list. How did you come into possession of it?" Blevins asked.

Twitch tensed.

"I understand The Arsenal is an officially recognized contractor of the FBI," Jennifer said, her gaze narrowed. "They provided the list to you."

"Your client had knowledge of the list. I'd like to know how."

"We don't always get what we want, Agent Blevins," Jennifer said.

"Very well." She took another sip of coffee, then looked down. "How well did you know Chastity?"

"We weren't very close. She approached me after the classes I taught. We chatted quite a few times."

"About?"

"Where are you going with this?" Jennifer asked.

"Did you ever see Chastity with anyone else? Perhaps a roommate, or a friend?" Agent Blevins asked.

Angie shook her head. "No, not that I recall, but I didn't pay much attention if I'm being entirely honest. Why?"

Fuck. They'd found something. Twitch glanced down at his phone when it pinged. A text from Ethan drew his attention.

Arsenal found Chastity's roommate has an SUV that matches.

"You've done a remarkable job staying alive against incredible odds, but this situation is going to take a more qualified skillset to get answers," Blevins said. "The Arsenal's involvement will speed up the investigation because they have the time and resources I wouldn't be able to devote to this as quickly."

Angie swallowed. Twitch watched the movement along her throat. "What now?"

"Now I continue investigating as under the radar as I can manage while you stay safe." Blevins glanced at Twitch. "What's the status from your end?"

"Claude wants a meeting with her," Twitch said. "He wants her. That's the real motivation."

"He's run my dojo for six months," Angie argued. "Of course we have to meet."

"Over dinner?" Twitch chuckled. "You aren't stupid, Angie. You know he wants more than a meeting."

"She should meet with Claude," Blevins said. "You can mic her. Drones are up in the dojo. Zoey said an Arsenal team had put up surveillance there and around the neighborhood. They're also putting them up at Claude's apartment and Chastity's."

"And you're okay with that?" Ethan asked. "I'm a bit surprised they'd admit that."

"They're federal contractors. They have more freedom to operate within the gray than I do, Mr. Davenport. My relationship with The Arsenal is complicated. I've learned to accept they'll cut corners whenever they can to keep people safe. I have no issues with that as long as it doesn't hinder prosecution."

"And it wouldn't," Jennifer said. "Every surveillance camera put up either has the property owner's permission or is public property."

"Exactly," Blevins said. "As I said, they cut corners we cannot because, even though they are contractors for us at times, they are legally an intermediary hired by Ms. Bierman. Their work on her behalf isn't within my purview."

Twitch chuckled. He doubted the FBI appreciated a private group with The Arsenal's clout inserting themselves into an active investigation. It was a complicated maze to navigate.

"And Wints?" Ethan asked.

"That's already in place," Blevins said. "Anyone with the slightest motivation has eyes on them right now. A meeting with Claude could give us the opportunity to determine his involvement, if there is one."

Twitch didn't want Angie meeting with Claude alone. The man's interest was obvious. Then again, he trusted Angie to hold her own against anyone. "Angie meeting with Claude alone is up to her. She's more than capable of defending herself against anyone, but she wouldn't be too far from protection either way."

"She'd be wired," Ethan said. "My only concern is the hacking aspect. Someone was skilled enough to penetrate the safe house's first layer of security."

"True." Blevins leaned her forearms on the table and crossed them. "Zoey explained that the first layer was an intentional trap designed for decent hackers. Now that they're aware there's a potential hacker involved, it won't happen again."

"Patch is working with Zoey to see if they can find the hacker's signature in other known hacks," Ethan said. "I don't pretend to understand it all, but I know my guy's working that angle with another person at The Arsenal."

"Jacob," Blevins said. "Recent addition, Judson Jensen's nephew. I believe you met them both briefly."

Twitch grunted. He remembered the scrawny geek who'd knocked him and Jud out with darts from a drone.

Ethan chuckled. "We've met."

"I understand there's a potential safe house nearby," Blevins said.

Twitch clenched. He doubted The Arsenal would've mentioned the network to an FBI agent, which meant the woman was likely fishing for information. He regarded Ethan across the table. The man's lips thinned.

The woman studied them both, but remained silent.

"Mr. Davenport has a lot of financial resources thanks

to Counterstrike," Angie said. "He must have secured a place to keep me safe. He did in San Antonio."

"Right," Blevins said. "Your organization is very impressive, Mr. Davenport. You and your brother have done tremendous work. How did you become involved with The Arsenal? Their paths don't exactly cross a group like yours in their day-to-day operations. Or am I mistaken?"

Ethan's jaw twitched. "Nolan Mason's Delta team recovered me from captivity. He saved my life."

"Ah, I must have overlooked that connection," Blevins said. "My apologies."

"As for The Arsenal's involvement with Counterstrike, if you've met any of the Masons, you'd know they are great operatives, but they're even better men," Ethan said. "They aren't the type of men to turn their backs on women and children who need help out of a violent situation."

"Yes. They somehow stumble across quite a few of those situations." Blevins smiled at the waitress who refilled her coffee. She picked up a sugar packet and dumped it into the coffee. "A suspicious person might think they somehow hunted for those specific problems."

"We wouldn't know anything about that," Jennifer said.

"We aren't Arsenal," Twitch said. "They do their thing, we do ours. Sometimes we find ourselves in need of more personnel to keep our clients safe. We engage their services when that situation arises."

"Fair enough," Blevins said. She looked over at Angie. "I'm curious. How exactly did you hear about Counterstrike? They're a small, locally-based organization. You were in Chicago."

"How is that relevant?" Jennifer asked.

"I need to firm up the timeline," Blevins answered. "Your client moved from one city to another alone. Until Chicago, where she somehow moved directly into Counterstrike's protection. That's a very large gray area I need to clear up to keep the case against whoever's guilty rock solid."

"How would that be a problem?" Twitch asked.

Jennifer's jaw twitched. "A defense attorney could use loopholes against prosecution. They'd likely offer a jury a plausible alternative to who was after her."

"If someone was helping her run, they could've had an ulterior motive that would weaken the case against the truly guilty party," Blevins said. "This is housecleaning. Nothing more, Ms. Bierman. I just need to understand how you came into contact with Counterstrike."

"I fled from a lot of cities, Agent Blevins," Angie said. "I'll admit I didn't have much of a strategy at first. I went wherever was closest and biggest and cheapest to get to at first. I figured I could hide easier in a large city than in a small town. After Atlanta, I realized I needed a better plan."

"That must've been expensive, moving through ten cities in six months. Your savings was depleted well before you left Atlanta," Blevins said.

They'd pulled Angie's financials. Twitch glared at Ethan, then Jennifer. They needed to shut this down. Fast.

Jennifer leaned forward. "Ms. Bierman doesn't owe

you any explanations about her financial situation unless it pertains to the investigation. Does it?"

Blevins ignored Jennifer altogether. "Not many women in that situation would have managed as well as you did, Angie."

"I was lucky."

"No, you were far more than lucky," Blevins said. "You were smart, strategic. You kept fighting and defending yourself. You remained focused and didn't let the fear and desperation incapacitate you. That's admirable."

"Whoever is after me underestimated me," Angie said. "That was their first mistake. As for the financial aspect of my flight, I admit I was running low on funds. My father taught me to always have cash on hand in case it was needed. I had enough with that and my savings to survive longer than I expected."

"Again, very smart."

Twitch suspected the woman admired Angie but was also playing her in hopes of getting more information. He narrowed his gaze but remained silent. Angie wasn't stupid enough to give anything away. She understood how important the network was. Agent Blevins couldn't find out about it. Too many relied on its anonymity and ability to operate outside the boundaries of the law when necessary.

"As for how I found Counterstrike, I used computers at libraries and coffee shops a lot like this one whenever I could." Angie motioned to the free computers along the side wall.

"In Chicago?" Blevins asked.

"Yes," Angie answered.

"Do you remember which one?"

"Don't answer that," Jennifer said. "Unless I'm mistaken, my client isn't under investigation. I don't see how this is relevant."

"How your client came into contact with a locally run organization like Counterstrike while in Chicago is a valid question that will come into question later," Blevins argued. "If you obtained assistance from anyone, I need to know, Ms. Bierman."

"It's amazing what you can find on the Internet when you're running for your life and desperate for any help you can find," Angie said. "I figured Texas was big and had a lot of large cities. When I searched Texas and local assistance resources, Counterstrike came up in the search. Specifically, an article about a woman named Marisol. Apparently, Counterstrike's efforts to help her from her abusive ex-husband made quite a few headlines."

Ethan glanced down at his phone and typed. Twitch suspected he was alerting Zoey to what Angie had just said. If anyone could provide a "trail" substantiating Angie's statement, it was The Arsenal.

"Taking down a bunch of corrupt police officers tends to do that," Twitch commented with a grin. Angie thought fast on her feet.

"Once again, your remarkable ability to think and act well under pressure is impressive, Ms. Bierman." Agent Blevin's gaze cut to Ethan. "As is Counterstrike's ability to help people who need it most. When this situation is resolved, I hope you know I'll gladly help you with future problems should the need arise. I might be an FBI agent, Mr. Davenport, but I'm a woman first and foremost. I lost a good friend to a violent bastard. I wish a group like yours would've been around to help her when the badge I wear wouldn't allow me to do what should've been done."

"We help anyone who needs it," Ethan said. "We'd appreciate your assistance in the future, should the need arise. Thank you."

Jennifer rose from the table. "Thank you, Agent Blevins. Please let us know what you find."

"Yes. And let me know how the meeting goes this evening."

CHAPTER 15

Angie kept quiet as the two equally silent men walked on either side of her. The crisp breeze brushed across her face as they made their way across the narrow street adjacent to the dojo. Ethan clicked the locks open. She slid into the backseat with Jennifer while both the men climbed into the front. The driver's side backseat door opened and Hazard slid in.

Silence maintained dominance as the vehicle slid from the curb and into the traffic. Okay, what the heck had just happened?

"You did well in there, Angie," Ethan commented, thereby breaking the tense silence.

Dread seeped within her. "She suspects something about the network, doesn't she?"

"Seems like it," Twitch answered.

"You did well," Jennifer said. "I wouldn't have thought to use the media coverage on Marisol's situation as an answer."

Angie peered out the window as the vehicle stopped at

a traffic light. She hoped it was enough to appease Agent Blevins. The woman seemed like the determined type who wouldn't give up easily.

"I take it the sit down wasn't a typical taking of a statement," Hazard said.

"Not at the end," Ethan said. "She was more curious about our involvement with The Arsenal and how Angie came to find what she saw as a local-only nonprofit. Fortunately, Angie here is a fast thinker and used media coverage about our takedown of the APD officers as how she came to know about Counterstrike."

The vehicle continued forward along the congested road. Angie didn't deserve praise for the answer. "Twitch mentioned what had happened. It seemed like a good enough excuse."

"We'll discuss our options for tonight in a minute. Right now we need a debrief with Zoey." Ethan glanced back at her. "Are you okay with that?"

"Yes. They need to know she's suspicious."

Angie kept quiet as Ethan called The Arsenal. Nervousness seeped through her. She didn't want the network jeopardized because of her. The FBI agent had become aware of its possible existence because she'd somehow gotten into Counterstrike's protective custody even though she was in Chicago.

"Ethan." Zoey's voice sounded worried. "Why are you calling? Didn't you meet with Agent Blevins?"

Jennifer offered a comforting smile as their gazes locked. A stack of paperwork filled the woman's lap. Angie wondered how many other cases she was handling.

"We did. A few concerns crept up. She was curious

about Counterstrike's involvement with The Arsenal and how Angie came into contact with us." Ethan turned right onto another road.

"Are you kidding me?"

"No, afraid not. Angie said she found Counterstrike through an Internet search at a coffee shop in Chicago," Twitch said.

"On it," Zoey said. "It'll take about half an hour, but I'll get a search history to that effect on a computer somewhere near the motel she was at. What else?"

Angie tried to remember the names of any local coffee shops or internet places near where she'd stayed but couldn't recall any. Hopefully Zoey would figure out possible venues.

"She mentioned other suspects and asked me about people who may have come to the dojo with Chastity," Angie said.

"Chastity and Hannah worked at the same place. Chastity's former roommate has an SUV that was on the DMV list of potential plate numbers," Zoey said. "I didn't think Blevins would've gotten that information yet, though. HERA literally spit it out just a few hours ago."

"She's good," Twitch commented. "Thorough."

Angie had no idea the two women had worked together, and a roommate made so much sense. Why hadn't she thought of that angle?

Because you were running for your life.

"Which is why we pulled strings to get her on the case," Zoey said. "Claude is under suspicion, too. Statements taken from Hannah's coworkers at the strip joint she used to work at mentioned she'd been seeing him."

"Why are we just now hearing about this?" Jennifer asked.

"No clue. It was buried within the statements the Philadelphia police had, though," Zoey said. "Let's rewind to what she asked about us and Angie."

Ethan gave Zoey a rundown of the conversation they'd had. On the surface level, none of it seemed too bad, but Angie learned long ago to prepare for the worst-case scenario. It was her father's mantra—one clearly shared by Zoey and Counterstrike.

By the time the woman was debriefed, the vehicle was on the highway and heading toward the safe house, or so she assumed. What if Chastity and Claude wanted to know where she was staying?

"What's wrong, Angel?" Twitch half-turned in the seat.

Surprise filled her at how easily he used the nickname in front of his boss. She didn't want him to get into trouble. She glanced at Ethan, who watched them, worry evident on his face.

"What if Claude or Chastity ask where I'm staying?"

"I was about to mention that." Twitch pulled out an address and handed it to her, along with a disposable phone. "This is the address you'll give them. It's a secondary location Medina's team is watching. It has drones up. If anyone hits it, we'll know."

Angie's gut tightened. They'd though ahead to have a trap location in place. She texted the address to Claude's cell, which had already been programmed into the disposable phone. "You were already ten steps ahead."

"That's what we do," Ethan commented. "Medina and his team got your safe house situated, as well as their nearby one. Then they got this third location up to use as a dummy location. It'll be provided to the Philadelphia police when they contact Jennifer for an address."

"I'll text Detective Shuler the information now," Jennifer said as she took the address from Angie. "Are you thinking someone's getting information from the police department?"

"It's a possibility," Twitch said.

A vehicle honked behind them as Ethan darted into the far-left lane. He navigated his way in and out of the traffic as though he'd lived in the area his entire life. His voice remained calm when he spoke. "We also have surveillance up at Angie's old apartment complex."

"Why?" Angie asked.

"I want to know if someone goes there looking for you," Ethan said.

Angie nodded and settled back into her seat. Of course, Twitch and Counterstrike had already factored in security. Chastity wouldn't be any threat when facing Counterstrike and The Arsenal. "I still can't believe either Chastity or Claude could be involved. I should've thought about close friends and family and acquaintances when I looked at the DMV records. I got so laser focused on Noah Wints when I saw his name that I didn't consider there'd be more than one hit."

"We almost missed it, too," Zoey said. "If Jacob hadn't been bitching about his dorm mate stealing his video console, I wouldn't have thought of it. Cruz's contacts in the Philadelphia office were so emphatic about Noah Wints being extremely accommodating and having a rock-solid alibi for when Hannah was murdered, though, that we figured there had to be a deeper connection somewhere. This doesn't absolve Noah, Angie. It just means we need to be extra cautious and keep our minds open to the possibility someone else might be guilty."

Right. Her friend, the man she'd entrusted her dojo to, could have killed Hannah. Hurt Chastity.

Hunted Angie.

"That circles us back to tonight. Claude wanted a private meeting with Angie to go over dojo business." Twitch tapped his knuckles against the window. "Agent Blevins believes we should let that happen and watch."

"We could contain the environment easily enough and keep her safe," Zoey said. "Angie? What do you think?"

Angie was grateful they thought to ask her. "I wish I could say firmly Claude isn't guilty, but I can't. We need to do this. It'd help clear a potential suspect. Right?"

"It would," Hazard said. "Are we thinking the dojo as the place?"

Angie had almost forgotten the quiet man beside her was in the vehicle.

"That's what she'd suggested when they spoke," Twitch said. "I'd just surprise the hell out of him and leave them alone to talk business."

"Okay, that leaves Chastity. We noticed she approached you on the way to your meeting with Agent Blevins. I say approached because she'd been in her vehicle for a while."

"Waiting," Ethan said. "Could her injuries have been self-sustained?"

She'd been waiting? Angie didn't like the unease filling her at the thought. Chastity was another person she'd trusted, taken at face value. How many others had she overlooked as potential threats?

"No," Zoey answered. "We've reviewed the medical records. There was significant facial damage and a cracked rib. Mild concussion. The stab wound was to the center of her abdomen, so it didn't puncture any organs, and she was raped. Bruising was indicative of forced sexual activity. The injuries were real."

Angie squeezed her eyes shut a moment and willed the visuals created by Zoey's words away. The anger and accusation in the woman's face at the hospital still haunted Angie.

"Hard to believe a woman who was attacked like that would be involved in it," Hazard said.

"We can't leave any possibility out until we have evidence to the contrary," Jennifer said. "Drop me off at the hotel by the apartment complex, Ethan. I want to get to work on following up with the Philly police."

The woman shoved all the paperwork back into her briefcase and pulled out her phone. She tapped a message, then stowed the device in her purse. Did she ever take a moment to do nothing more than rest?

"Okay," Ethan said. "Do we need to put someone on Chastity, Zoey?"

"Someone on Medina's team is following her," Zoey said. "Someone else is staying with Claude since you three have Angie secured."

What about Noah? Was anyone still worried about him?

"You're thinking something really hard right now, Angie." Hazard's quiet tone matched his demeanor.

"What about Noah?"

"He has a rock-solid alibi for Hannah's attack," Zoey said.

"I know he had an alibi, but I still don't understand why he suddenly got into touch with me to train him. Agent Blevins was right. There are far better instructors out there that he could have hired," Angie said.

"As a billionaire myself, I can admit that, if I were single, I'd hire a beautiful female martial arts expert over some ugly-faced male any day," Ethan said. "We can't forget that he's a horny, rich bastard. Sometimes the motivation is as simple as that."

Compliments had always been hard to accept. Hearing them from strong, handsome men like Ethan always left her at a loss for words.

"Did he make a pass at you?" Twitch asked.

"Yeah, several." Angie looked out the window. "Most of the men who hire me for private sessions do, though. It's kind of an expected situation, to be honest."

"We have him under surveillance, Angie," Zoey said. "We're still digging into the corporation behind the payments, too. I find it hard to believe a martial arts instructor or a stripper would open a shell corporation and have the finances needed to hire the people who attacked you. That takes serious cabbage, not to mention connections."

Angie recalled the conversations she'd had with Claude right after Noah hired her. "He referenced the rich life, mentioned caviar breakfasts and personal jets and choppers. He mentioned the lack of privacy because bodyguards were always around."

"Who did? Wints?" Ethan asked.

"No." Angie swallowed. "Claude. Right after Noah hired me, Claude mentioned stuff like that several times. When I asked how he'd know, he said he used to bodyguard for a company that hired out to protect rich people."

"We've started diving into his past. We'll find out who all he's associated with soon enough," Zoey said.

Angie was tired of not having answers. She'd fled, fought to stay alive for six months. She couldn't imagine someone she'd trusted being behind the attacks, but what if they were?

"Medina stayed back at one of the apartments we secured so he could monitor the surveillance. He just messaged that Angie's dad is at her old place."

"How does he know she's back?" Ethan asked.

"He's INSCOM. He likely has her name flagged," Zoey said. "I can have Medina pull him out."

"I want to see him." Angie's voice rose.

"I'll have Medina take him to the real safe house, then," Twitch said. He pulled out his phone.

Everyone she'd trusted in Philly was in question now. She didn't know who to believe or trust other than Twitch and Counterstrike. And The Arsenal. She needed contact with someone from before all this mess started.

She wanted her family.

Ethan stopped to let Jennifer out at a hotel, then they maneuvered back onto the highway. About fifteen minutes later, the vehicle pulled into a parking spot beside an apartment building. Although she wanted to unlatch her seatbelt and scramble into her place to see her dad, she waited patiently as Hazard, Ethan, and Twitch exited first. She remained where she was until Twitch motioned for her to exit.

He grasped her face and kissed her. The soft, brief contact wasn't nearly enough. She sank into his arms and sighed wearily. "Tell me this is almost over."

"I wish I could," he whispered into her hair. "We'll figure this out. I know it's hard to hear they might be involved."

"I don't know who to trust anymore. I never made friends easily. Claude was one of the few I trusted here. And Chastity..." She shivered in Twitch's arms. "I don't see how she could be involved after what happened to her. It doesn't make any sense to me."

"We'll get answers." He lifted her head by her chin and smiled. "Come on. I'm thinking your dad saw us pull up. I'm surprised he isn't out here shoving me out of the way."

He was likely cleaning his guns to shoot Twitch the moment he walked in. There wasn't any way her dad would fail to see her interest in the man who held her close.

"Is this the real safe house?" Angie asked.

"Yes, a two-bedroom apartment. It's fully furnished and will be yours until we get this mess resolved."

Emotion clogged her throat as Twitch wrapped an arm around her and they headed into the safe house. The dam she'd held a firm grip on exploded the moment she saw her father. She walked straight to him and fell into his arms.

"Dad." A sob escaped her.

"It's okay, Angel Eyes." He kissed her temple and

gripped her tight. Emotion broke his words. “Is there a reason my girl’s sobbing?”

“She’s had a rough afternoon,” Twitch said. “I’m John Stanz, with Counterstrike. Or Twitch.”

“Right. You’re the primary on my girl’s protection. I saw you’ve got a vested interest in her safety now. We’ll be having words about that later,” her dad said.

Not much escaped his notice. She couldn’t help but laugh. She blinked back the tears and separated from him. “What are you doing here?”

“I took some time off, decided to lay low at my place in case I was needed.” He draped an arm around her as he looked at each of the men. “Then I saw records being accessed and figured the investigation was honing in on a suspect. A friend of mine mentioned an FBI agent had been called in from DC, as a special favor to the Secretary of Defense. There’s only one group I know with the clout to make that happen.”

Ethan’s jaw twitched as he chuckled. “That’s a big favor to call in.”

“I’m sure Quillery and Edge have quite a few favors they can call in whenever they want. I’m glad they pulled that string for my girl,” her dad said. “I’m Adam Bierman, pleased to meet you all. I’ll stay out of the way, but I’d appreciate a read-in on what’s going on.”

“Of course,” Ethan said. “I’m Ethan Davenport. This is Hazard and Twitch. The Arsenal has a team here, but they’re perimeter only. Most are on surveillance detail on a couple of our suspects. Their leader tagged your entry and let us know you were here.”

“Ah, so that’s your tech I spotted. One heck of a setup.

I figure there's not a speck of interior or exterior not covered. Am I right?"

"That's the hope," Twitch said. "I'm glad you are here, sir, but I'm afraid we're low on time and have a lot of ground to cover in a short timeframe. Ethan can get you up to speed while Hazard and I get your daughter ready for tonight."

"Tonight?" Her father's eyebrows furrowed.

"Counterstrike and The Arsenal think Claude might be involved somehow. He wants to meet with me privately to discuss the dojo and what all has happened since I've been gone. I'm taking the meeting after tonight's class," Angie said. "I'll be wired and protected, but we're hoping to get some answers and hopefully determine his involvement, if any."

Her father grunted. "I'll chat with Ethan. You two keep my girl safe. I'll want a detailed debrief once there's time."

Emotion filled her dad's face when he touched her hair. She put her hand atop his and blinked back the new wave of tears coming forth. "Thanks for coming, Dad."

"I wish I'd known this mess was going on sooner. It breaks my heart to see my girl in trouble and not be able to stop it."

"We'll talk later, when I get home. You're staying with me, right?"

"We'll see. I don't want to get in the way of keeping you safe. That's the primary objective here."

Angie smiled. Ever the soldier. "Love you, Dad."

"Love you too, Angel Eyes."

CHAPTER 16

An awkward silence loomed within the dojo when the last of the class participants departed. Angie wondered for a moment where Chastity had gone because they were supposed to talk after the cool down ended. But she wasn't Angie's problem tonight. Someone was following her.

"You're doing great, Angie," Twitch said, his voice strong and confident in her ear. The tiny earbud he'd given her was so comfortable she'd almost forgotten she wore one.

Claude finished cleaning the floor and set the mop aside. His gaze swept the empty room, then he approached. Unease tightened her insides. She hated the fact she'd grown to distrust the man who'd been so instrumental in helping the dojo succeed.

Although she'd poured her heart and soul into its creation, Claude had helped turn it into the success it was. He'd been at her side most of the time.

"Where's the caveman?"

"Twitch. His name is Twitch. He knew we had business to discuss."

"Business." The man spat the word like a curse. "Is that all I am? Business?"

"Claude, you know I'm not interested in you like that. I'm sorry, but that isn't ever happening between us." She kept her voice firm and normal despite the hard thud of her heart. Surveillance drones were in position throughout the dojo.

Twitch and Hazard had shown her maps of her dojo and the entire neighborhood. They'd run over potential exit scenarios repeatedly until she felt confident about their locations and all possible ways out of the situation. If she got into trouble, the drones would dart whoever threatened her and she had multiple ways out of the dojo —all of which were covered by either Counterstrike or Arsenal personnel. She was safe.

And alone with a man she'd once trusted but everyone suspected was somehow involved in her ordeal. She sat at the folding table they used as a sign-up area and met Claude's intense glare with one of her own when he sat across from her.

No. She wasn't alone. Twitch was on the com in her ear. He and Counterstrike and The Arsenal were all watching via the drones.

"Shouldn't we do this in the office?" Claude asked.

"I dunno. You tell me." She placed her hand atop the other and fought the urge to shake him. "What would you like to discuss first?"

"You should've told me you were leaving, Angie. I could have helped you."

"It was safer for everyone this way. I couldn't risk anyone I cared for getting hurt." She lowered her voice. "You did a great job while I was away. Thank you."

"Don't thank me," he growled. "You shouldn't have left. You were safer here with me than out there alone."

Her gut tightened. "You don't know that. You have no idea what I went through after I left. Do you?"

"Of course not. You never called me." He pounded the table. Pens splattered to the floor.

Her pulse quickened. Claude was a great guy, but had one hell of a temper. "Claude, don't. You know I don't handle your rage issues well. Control your shit or I'll kick your ass."

"Rage issues?" Zoey asked. "Why am I just now hearing about that?"

"Good question," Twitch growled.

"You promised you were taking your medicine," Angie said.

"I am." Claude stood and swiped a hand through his hair. "I'm sorry. I've got it under control."

"Good." Angie swallowed, forced the conversation forward. "Claude, I need to ask you something and I want an honest answer. You owe me that."

"You're the one who owes me for keeping this place open, but fine. What do you want to know?"

"I met with the FBI today," Angie said.

"What the fuck? Why?" The man's gaze widened. He came around the table and stood just outside her strike range. "Why did you go to the FBI?"

"Someone's hunting me across state lines. They hacked

into a federally protected security system. Why wouldn't I go to the FBI?"

"Fuck. They can't help with this, Angie. That wasn't smart." Claude paced.

"You were involved with Hannah."

Shock registered in the man's gaze. "Did your caveman tell you that?"

"Say yes," Twitch said. "We don't want him knowing the FBI is investigating him already. He panicked hearing you went to them."

"I'm on it," Zoey said. "Something tells me Claude has a dirty background HERA isn't finding for some reason. Son of a bitch, facial recognition only goes back two years."

"How did we not know this before?" Twitch asked.

"Because Claude's involvement with Hannah didn't come to light until last night, big man," Zoey answered.

Hearing an entire conversation in her ear was weird. Angie realized she'd remained quiet too long when Claude took a step toward her. "Yes, Twitch told me. Apparently, it wasn't too difficult to find out. Why didn't you tell me?"

"It wasn't your business. It's not like you wanted anything to do with me outside this fucking place." He looked away. "Jesus, Angie. None of this should've happened. This was a clean break for me, a fresh start. How did everything get so fucked up?"

A fresh start?

"That's not good," Zoey said. "Everyone move into the first strike position. Our man's got a background. I'm digging, but I'm not liking his tone."

"Neither am I," Twitch said.

Angie's heart thundered in her chest. She moved around the table so she had a clear strike zone. The less objects around her, the better. Claude followed her progression deeper into the room.

"Why are you asking about her?"

"She was murdered! That's what started this whole nightmare for me, Claude. I deserve an answer. What happened with Hannah?"

"What always happens."

"Which is?"

"You wouldn't understand." He ran his hand through his hair and started pacing. His long legs chewed up the floor. Back and forth. "Fuck."

"Keep him talking, Angie. We need more time," Zoey said. Her voice drifted off. "Jacob, I need you combing the data coming out. I reprogrammed the facial recognition program to pull similarities above seventy percent instead of ninety-five."

"What the fuck did you tell the FBI?"

"I told them about the attacks, being hunted like an animal. Why are you so worried about them?"

"You shouldn't have involved them. I could've helped you."

"How? Claude, please. Help me understand. You aren't making any sense." She took a step forward. "Please. Tell me about Hannah. Whatever it is, we'll sort it out. I'll help."

"Fuck Hannah, Angie. She's not the problem. She wasn't ever anything more than an itch I scratched when I couldn't deal with the blue balls you left me with every fucking day." Red rose in his face. He expended a loud breath. "Look, I know this looks bad, but I can fix it. Okay? I can make all of this go away if you trust me."

"He wants to protect you, like you're a weak woman who needs a strong man," Zoey said. "Appeal to that nature. That'll get him to open up."

Right. Hapless female. Okay, she could do that. Maybe.

"You're scaring me," Angie said. "I'm tired, Claude. I'm sick and tired of the running and being terrified out of my fucking skull. Now I'm finally back home. Here. With you. Then I find out you were involved with Hannah? Why did you hide that? Did you kill her?"

"No! What the fuck? Why would you even think that?" He ran his hand through his hair again. "Fuck, this is so screwed up. This wasn't supposed to happen."

"Claude, you aren't making any sense." Angie suspected Twitch and everyone else listening in would lose their patience soon if he didn't start explaining what the hell was going on.

"Before I came here, I worked for a family, doing enforcement and protective work mostly." He glanced at her. "I'm not proud of the things I did, Angie."

"Narrow the search you're running on the results, Jacob. Organized crime. Drugs. Trafficking," Zoey said. "You're doing great, Angie. Keep him talking. Every little detail he gives helps narrow the search parameters down."

"We all do things we aren't proud of sometimes," Angie said. She kept her body relaxed, but mentally prepared in case she had to defend herself. "Did you know her before you came to Philly?"

"No. She was sweet, like an innocent angel who wanted to get dirty," Claude said.

Revulsion rolled through her when she remembered Hannah's fear. "She was scared of someone before she died. Did she talk to you about it?"

"She tried. I didn't give a shit. All I wanted was a clean break. I didn't want to get mixed up in her shit when I'd barely escaped my own." Claude's haunted expression startled Angie. "I came here on impulse. I'd heard about this place, heard the local neighborhood kids talking about a new ninja master or some stupid shit like that. You were supposed to be the balance, you know. A way to undo the fucked-up shit I'd done."

"Whatever it was you did couldn't have been that bad. We've all done things to get by. Hell, I've killed people, Claude." Her voice spiked. "I have blood on my hands. Men who probably didn't even know what they were hiring on for. Or why."

"They weren't innocent, Angie," he growled.

"How would you know?"

"Innocent men don't hire on to hurt a woman." He spat the claim. "I know. I was just like them. Worse."

"Claude, whatever you did, we can work through it."

"There's never an out, not with the family I worked for," he said. "But the old man understood the troubles I had and let me walk, said it was a gift for the exceptional work I'd done."

"What troubles?" Angie asked, keeping her mind on the task at hand rather than the chaotic emotions rolling through her.

"His daughter had problems, got interested in me. I

tried like hell to scrape her off, Angie. I swear to Christ I did." Claude's voice rose. "But she wouldn't stop. It was endless. I'd come back to my pad after doing horrible shit that made me puke afterward and she'd be naked in my bed, handcuffed to it. Begging me to do twisted shit to her."

Dread settled in her. Horrible shit that made him puke afterward? Twisted shit?

"I never touched her, Angie. Not. Once." He ran a hand down his face.

"Who didn't you touch? The daughter?"

"Yeah. Fuck, she was persistent. She got off on pain—couldn't ever get hurt enough."

"Tell me we have enough to get her out of there," Twitch growled.

"Stand down. She's got this under control," Zoey ordered.

"She needed help, Claude. That's not your fault. You were a good man not to take advantage," Angie said.

"I went to the old man after dealing with it for over a year. He promised it'd stop and it got worse."

"Claude..." She wasn't sure what to say.

"I got away. I hopped into my car and drove off the second the old man said I could. It was the scariest two hours of my life, Angie. Fuck. I just knew the old man would send a crew to end me. I didn't deserve a clean start, not after the shit I'd done. But I got it. I drove down here to Philly and found your dojo a week later. It was everything I needed." The haunted expression in his face startled her. "You were everything I needed and so much more."

"Got him," Zoey said. The com went silent.

Got him? What did that mean? Trusting Twitch and Zoey to handle whatever was going on, she focused on Claude and what he's said. She was everything he'd needed and more.

She shook her head and took a step backward.

"Jesus, Angie. I'd never hurt you."

"Who was she?"

"I tried getting her away from here, you know. I knew she'd cause trouble when I saw her. I called the old man, but he said she wasn't his problem anymore. He'd scraped her off."

"Claude." She shouted his name. "Who?"

The man was lost in the memories, though. "I'd met Hannah, gotten things going with her for a couple weeks. She was sweet and so fucking lost because of that bastard Eric. We were two lost souls just trying to find our way. That's what she said."

His voice softened when he talked about her. Angie clutched her stomach, willed patience she didn't have. She wanted answers, but the man's torment whipped through the room like a thunderstorm.

"I was picking her up at work one night. I'd gone in to check out her last show. That's when I saw the bitch and knew my fresh start wasn't clean. She'd followed me."

Oh. My. God.

"Chastity." Angie breathed the name.

"I begged her to leave Hannah be. I didn't think that bitch had that level of crazy in her, Angie. I swear to Christ I didn't know or I would've handled her myself." Tears trekked down his cheeks. "I didn't even believe it was her when Hannah was found. Chastity came to me, terrified. Said some of her father's enemies were after her and her friends and that's why Hannah was dead. I believed her."

"You never said anything." Anger spiked in Angie. "You knew this the entire time and didn't say a damn thing."

"I didn't know a damn thing! Don't you see? The crazy bitch had her father's men beat and rape her! That's the shit she was into. I should have known she'd done it, but I didn't. I didn't want to believe I was twisted up with that kind of whack job."

"Claude, you have to go to the police and tell them this. They need to know."

"I can't. Look, I'm smarter now. I can keep you safe from her. I've got her under control."

"How? You had her pack up my apartment with you. That's not something you do with someone you say is crazy."

"I can control her, Angie. After you left, I realized she must've had something to do with Hannah. I can keep her calm. I ran 'cause I was sick of her shit, but for you I'll deal with it."

"Claude, I think you're the crazy one. How could you think I'd be okay with you controlling Chastity if she murdered someone?" Was she the one who'd sent people to attack her? "Did she send people after me? How?"

"None of that matters now, Angie," Claude said. "If she gives you anymore trouble, we'll go somewhere, hideout. I've got more than enough money stashed to keep us secure."

"For fuck's sake, Zoey," Twitch growled into the com.

"Angie, I need you to remain calm. Agent Blevins is going to enter with police officers. And Twitch. We have what we need to arrest Claude. We'll explain everything once he's in custody, okay?"

Angie nodded, knowing they'd see her movement on the drones. Sourness coated her stomach. "I'm not running away with you. Why would you think I would? You knew she might've killed Hannah and you never went to the police. There's an innocent man facing murder charges because of her. And you."

"I didn't have anything to do with what Chastity did," Claude argued.

Angie shook her head. "Saying nothing is the same as helping her."

The door to the dojo opened. Claude spun to face the group of people walking in. Angie's eyes burned as turmoil overtook her. Anger and empathy vied for control. Agent Blevins closed the distance between herself and Claude.

"What did you do?" Claude asked. "I didn't do anything wrong. I didn't know it was her until you'd already ran."

"FBI." Agent Blevins flashed a badge as two police officers drew their weapons and aimed them at Claude. "Hollis Madelone, you're under arrest for extortion, narcotics trafficking, and murder."

Claude lunged for Angie. She kicked, aiming for a hard strike just below his knee. He screamed as he fell.

"You stupid bitch! What did you do? I wanted to protect you!"

Hollis Madelone? Angie took several steps backward as the police took the man she'd known as Claude into custody. Confusion kept her silent a moment. Twitch and Ethan approached.

"Why's he being arrested for murder? He said it was Chastity, not him," Angie said.

"He's not being arrested for her murder," Twitch said. He put an arm around her. "It took HERA a while to identify him because he's had a lot of facial surgeries, but Claude is actually Hollis Madelone, a wanted fugitive who worked for the Carlini crime family."

"You're making a mistake," Claude said. He glared at Angie. "I just wanted a fresh start. You've gotta understand. I'm just as much a victim as you are. She's nuts. Her whole family is. I had to get away."

"Murder. Extortion." Tears burned her eyes as she stared at the man struggling in the policeman's grasp. "You can't start clean if you don't wash away what you walked away from. You're better than the life you led. Now you have the chance to prove that. Help them, Claude."

In a way she'd tried doing the same thing when she'd run from Philly. Guilt chewed her insides. She wasn't much better than Claude. Or Hollis. God, she'd never imagined he was anything more than a great man who'd become a friend.

"I wasn't a good man back then, but I've changed. I got out and started over." Regret filled his eyes. "I'll cooperate. For you and Hannah, I'll do the right thing."

Angie let the tears fall as they hauled him out. Agent Blevins moved to stand in front of her. The woman's lips thinned as she placed her hands on both hips. "I'll get him to talk and give us what he knows about Chastity. Carlini only had one daughter, Carly. We'll need to look into it more once we apprehend her for questioning, but she must have followed Madelone here."

"If she used Carlini's men to help her murder Hannah, would that implicate her father?" Twitch asked.

"Maybe." Her gaze slid between them. "That'll be above my head. I'm sure The Arsenal or the FBI geeks will trace the shell corporation to the Carlini family now that we're aware of their involvement."

"Zoey said there's a lot of federal interest in the Carlini family. They'll flip her," Ethan said as he approached. "And Madelone."

Anger spiked within Angie. She understood Claude getting a deal. From what he'd shared, the man had been trying to make a clean break. Chastity didn't deserve a deal. She'd killed Hannah and stalked Claude

"Six months of running, fighting assholes at every turn. It's hard to believe it might be over," Angie said, giving voice to the frustrations plaguing her. "I'm okay with Claude getting a deal, but Chastity needs to rot in prison."

"We'll need to see how things go once we have her in custody," Agent Blevins said. "There could be backlash from the Carlini family."

Twitch tensed beside her. "We aren't easing off the protective detail anytime soon."

"Good. I'll be in touch." The woman looked at Angie. "You did well tonight."

"I had a lot of help."

CHAPTER 17

Angie trembled. The shiver traveled clear to her bones and refused to vacate.

Shock.

She'd killed people and not had such a violent reaction in the aftermath. Why had seeing Claude arrested affected her so. "I trusted him."

The whispered explanation escaped her as she moved deeper into Twitch's arms. A curse escaped him as he wrapped the blanket tighter around her and kissed her temple.

"Hang on, Angel. I've got you."

Red and blue lights swirled, casting their bright auras outward into the inky darkness enveloping the neighborhood. Curious onlookers watched across the neighboring sidewalk.

"How is she?" Ethan asked.

"I'm fine," she lied. "Can we go?"

Nausea ensued whenever she glanced back at the dojo. God, she'd been so damn naive. She'd trusted Claude with her business and members. Kids. Abuse survivors. What if he'd hurt them?

"I'm taking her home, Agent Blevins," Twitch said, his words more of a declaration than a request for permission.

The woman turned. Her gaze swept over them both, but locked on to Angie. "I'll come by in a couple of hours."

"You'll come by in the morning," Ethan said. "It's late, our client is exhausted and in shock. Her legal counsel is asleep. Ms. Bierman isn't going anywhere."

"Right." The woman's gaze returned to Angie. "You did well in there. Get some rest. This is almost over."

She didn't know that. The man Angie knew as Claude had been an enforcer for a crime family. The daughter of said crime family's leader had killed Hannah and chased Angie across the country.

No.

She'd hired assholes who worked for her father to do it.

She'd overheard enough of what Claude, aka Hollis Madelone, said before he'd been hauled away to get the gist. Chastity was not only nuts, she was psychotic and intelligent enough to know exactly how to get her daddy's henchmen to do whatever she wanted—including hiring hackers to chase Angie's trail and local thugs to hunt her down.

Would they continue doing her bidding if she was behind bars?

The thought reactivated the part of herself she'd kept locked down for months. Fear.

She'd depleted her adrenaline reserves and was

running on the fumes of her courage. There was only so much a person could take, and she'd found her limit tonight.

"She should remain here, at least for the next half hour or so," Blevins said, her cell phone pressed to her ear. She leaned in and whispered something to Ethan.

The man tensed. Hands fisted, jaw twitching, the man pulled out his cell.

"What's wrong?" Angie asked, her voice high pitched in her ears. Her pulse quickened.

"Let's go," Ethan ordered. "Hazard's pulling the vehicle up."

Twitch lifted Angie. She wrapped her arms around her neck as he moved quickly toward the SUV that pulled up a few feet away. Ethan jumped into the front seat while Twitch slid her into the backseat, then got in beside her.

Hazard pulled away from the curb as Twitch was slamming the rear door closed. Ethan reached over to the console and punched a button. A ringing sounded through the speakers.

"A little busy right now," Medina said, his voice gruff.

"Tell me you got her."

Her? Angie's breath froze in her lungs.

"We got her," the man confirmed.

Angie breathed once again. The her had to be Chastity. Who else could it possibly be? She remained silent and scooted closer to Twitch. He wrapped his arm around her and kissed her forehead.

"We're on our way," Ethan said. "I'm going to drop Twitch and Angie off at the safe house first."

"Might be best to wait a while. Emergency services is

still here, so are the local cops and a few feds. I'm thinking the latter two groups will be here a while measuring their dicks to see who's got jurisdiction over this."

"What happened?" Twitch asked.

"HERA's drones flagged a group of people exiting a vehicle near the trap location. Real-time facial scans recognized them as Carlini henchmen. Chastity arrived moments later."

"How the hell did they get the location so quickly?" Twitch asked.

"Details are still coming in, but Zoey's assuming it was a payoff to someone at the police department. They're the only ones who had the address at this point, other than Claude."

Medina sighed heavily into the phone. "Not sure we should get into the rest over the phone. It's more of a face-to-face so you'd believe me kind of debrief."

"I'm thinking we'd rather hear it now," Ethan said. "Angie's had a rough enough day without dragging this out."

"Right. For the record, the rest of this was not our idea."

"What the fuck happened?" Twitch growled.

"I'll preface this with the fact that everyone is okay. The only injuries were to the combatants." Medina paused, but his words settled some of the worry inside her. "The initial order was for my team to establish contact once Chastity's henchmen breached what they assumed was Angie's safe house."

"Okay," Ethan said. "Sound plan."

"Right. Angie's father, who was with me, disagreed."

"Dad changed the plan. Didn't he?" Angie asked.

"He's a career military strategist," Medina explained unnecessarily.

Angie knew exactly what her father was. He wouldn't have let them be taken down inside an empty safe house. "That wouldn't have given authorities enough to charge them."

"You sound just like him." Medina chuckled. "We switched the play last second. Her father entered through the back door. The trap location was near enough to our real location for us to arrive in time to get him into position since the henchmen waited for Chastity to arrive. They breached the safe house and made contact with her father. My team and I moved in and took them into custody. Drones recorded the entire thing, including Chastity's presence and the orders she was shouting."

"They went after my father." Anger rose in Angie.

"It was a psychopath's Hail Mary. She hoped to find you there," Medina said. "The delay in reaction moved the charges into felonies."

"It also strengthened the case against Chastity," Ethan said. "Good work. Her father's okay?"

"He took a couple hits, just enough for good pictures." Medina laughed. "His words, not mine. I see where Angie gets her guts from."

"I want to go there, not to the safe house. I want to see my dad."

"Not sure that's a good idea, Angel. You've had a rough night," Twitch said.

"I want to see my dad," she repeated.

"We'll be there in a few." Ethan clicked off. He glanced back. "This is almost over."

Thank God. She relaxed against Twitch and focused on the beat of his heart against her ear. Just a little while longer and it'd all be over. Her life could return to normal.

But what was normal?

Claude had been an imposter. Chastity had been a murderer. Angie had almost vomited just looking at her dojo after she'd been led outside. Could she move on and put all of that behind her?

Did she even want to?

She burrowed deeper into the silent man running his fingers through her hair. He'd support whatever decision she made. The instinctive realization filled her, a balm to the agitation spewing its toxin into her thoughts.

No matter what she decided to do, she and Twitch would make their relationship work. Anything worth having was worth fighting for. The man she leaned against was worth any fight.

* * *

TWITCH HUNG TOWARD THE BACK OF THE LIVING ROOM OF the real safe house as Angie chatted with her father. She'd spent a good half hour fussing over the older man's blackening eye. She held an icepack in place, clearly not trusting him to do it himself.

"Jennifer and I are returning to Austin in the morning. She can handle the rest of her work for Angie from our offices," Ethan said. "I figure Hazard can hang out for another few days, just in case something comes up."

Twitch grunted. He'd hoped to hold this conversation off until the morning, but boss man clearly had a different timeline. "I'd like to use some vacation time, stay here a bit longer to make sure Angie's secured here."

"Take the time you need." Ethan shifted his stance and turned to face Twitch. "Hazard said he spoke with you, gave some advice about Bea and your mom."

"He doesn't understand the situation," Twitch said. "You and Milo have done a lot for me and my family. I'm not sure that's a debt I'll ever be able to repay."

"That's not a debt. It's a privilege. I'm glad we could help when Bea needed us," Ethan said. His voice lowered. "I'm hoping you'll let us do the same for you."

"I'll make this work. Counterstrike is important to me."

"So is Angie."

"I'll make this work," he repeated.

"Yeah, you will, but not alone. I've got an idea, one that might help. But I've got to know how serious you are about her and making it work."

Twitch chuckled. "Never in a million fucking years would I have imagined you asking my intentions toward a woman." He wasn't sure whether he wanted to admit what he'd yet to share with even Angie. He was falling in love. "She's a priority. I'm not walking away, even if that would be the right thing to do."

"Good." Ethan smiled. "I never realized how listless and colorless my life was until I fell in love with Mari. Every day is a new chapter, one I create with her. For her."

"Pleased as hell for you," Twitch said.

"Tomorrow, I'm sitting Angie down and offering her a

position within Counterstrike—one that'd give her the chance to help us establish dojos like the one she has here across the country. Safe refuges for people who need help."

"That's a great idea, man. Not sure she'd walk away from this place."

"She wouldn't have to. It'd be the first one. I want a brick and mortar facility that'll give people the help they need in every majority city," Ethan said. "She has the skillset to help make that dream a reality."

She did.

"I want you running it."

Shock struck Twitch. Ethan could have anyone he wanted running something that extensive and important. "I appreciate that, man. That hits me center mass that you'd offer me the job, but we both know there are a lot of people more qualified than me."

"Qualifications can be learned. I need someone I'd trust with anyone who walks into those facilities. Someone who gets why this is the most important thing we could possibly do. That's you." Ethan's stance shifted once more as he watched Angie. "Seeing her with those kids in San Antonio gutted me, man. She accomplished more in four hours than most people do in a lifetime for the people we need to reach."

"She can't be everywhere all the time. None of us can."

"No, but she can train others who possess the same spirit and abilities," Ethan said. "So can you. We started Counterstrike with the finances needed. The blood. The Arsenal has the network. The fiber and bone. Angie's the heart and you're the soul."

"That's downright poetic," Twitch teased with a chuckle.

"Think about it tonight. I wanted to make this happen before we sat down with Blevins earlier. Hearing her ask Angie how she got into contact with Counterstrike was another gut punch. What if she hadn't been at that bus stop and those two women hadn't called Ben? How many Angies are out there needing us and the network?"

Too many.

"I wonder what would've happened to Bea and Ryan if you and Milo hadn't been nearby and willing to help when I couldn't," Twitch said. "I'm in. Regardless of what Angie chooses, I'll do whatever I can to help. Though, she's the asset."

"You both are." Ethan sighed. "I haven't chatted with them about it yet, but I want to extend an offer with The Arsenal to assist us with this. Their tech and teams were a huge leg up with Angie's problems. We won't ever have the bandwidth to get operatives that well-trained. It'd take us years to get to that level. Our focus needs to remain on the clients."

"They're pretty loaded down with work."

"Yeah, but Medina mentioned there are a lot of operatives not on teams. Zoey and her bosses want to get them training in team-based situations. Our facilities would have those."

"It's a smart idea. I'd be on board. I'm sure everyone back at Counterstrike would be." Twitch smirked. "It'd give a fleshed out in-your-face presence to the network."

"That's the idea."

"Then let's make it happen," Twitch said.

* * *

"YOU'RE THINKING SO HARD I CAN HEAR IT ACROSS THE room."

Angie glanced over her shoulder at the gorgeous man sprawled on the double-sized bed. His feet dangled off the end but he either didn't care or was too exhausted to care. Sated bliss tingled through her body. Although it'd been a long, stressful day, she and Twitch had found the energy to make love in the shower and then again afterward on the bed.

"Come to bed, Angel."

She turned and headed toward the man who'd occupied her thoughts since they'd separated themselves from everyone hours ago. Exhaustion plagued her, but she wasn't willing to close her eyes and end the day because doing so meant they were a day closer to the end.

The end of her nightmare.

The end of the bliss she'd found with Twitch.

She curled into his arms and stretched her legs until they wound with his long, muscular ones. The worry threading through her bliss made its way into her voice. "Tell me we'll figure out a way to keep this going."

"No way in hell I'm giving you up," Twitch said. He wrapped his arm around her and cupped her face. "Is that why you've been staring out your balcony?"

"Partly. I'm worried about Dad. He's not going to take retirement well. He's not a sedentary personality."

"You take after him." Twitch smiled. "He'll figure it out. Though, the answer could be at your dojo. He could help you with it."

She'd lost Claude. The wound of that loss hadn't been visited, likely wouldn't for a while. "He'd be good with the kids. He taught me most of what I learned."

"I figured he had. I'm gonna warn you about something I probably shouldn't mention, but I'm not ever keeping secrets from you. This isn't a secret, but it is something Ethan wouldn't appreciate me discussing with you before he's had his say."

Angie firmed her grip on Twitch and glanced up. "I saw you two talking earlier when we first got back. It looked intense."

"He's got big plans. Those will involve you if he has his say. He wants a brick and mortar presence for Counterstrike and the network nationwide, all the big cities. Dojos like what you have here or community centers like he's constructing in San Antonio." Intensity resonated in his gaze. "He's gonna ask you to lead that endeavor, get people trained to teach self-defense and other classes like you do."

Wow. Angie swallowed as her mind shook off its exhaustion and started traveling the what-if trails. The potential for such a grand-scale endeavor was huge. Almost unending. "That sounds fantastic, Twitch, but I'm not sure I'm what he needs. I mean, a billionaire like him could get anyone he wanted. There are way more qualified people."

"He wants you." Twitch caressed her face with his thumb. "I'll be honest. He likely has ulterior motives because he asked me to help manage the locations. There'd be operatives available in the area to offer investigative and protective services like Counterstrike did with you. I know there's people way more qualified than me, which means he's strategizing a way to make it easier for you and I to stay together."

God. Warmth seeped into her. She stroked Twitch's jaw. "What did you say?"

"I'm in. Whatever your decision, I'm gonna be part of this. It's too important to not do what I can." Twitch feathered a kiss across her lips. "I'm not telling you this to pressure you, Angie. I'm gonna make this work with us no matter what you decide."

"What about your family? Your mom and sister?"

"Things are going to change. That's a discussion I've put off for a long time. Hazard and Ethan both knocked that fact across my head more than once recently." Twitch ran his fingers through her hair. "You're too important to not be my first priority, sweetheart. I know it's way too early, but I'm falling in love with you."

"John." His real name tumbled from her lips as the intensity of the moment impacted her. "I'm terrified because I'm falling in love with you too. This is crazy."

"Love doesn't operate on a timetable. It fights dirty and hits you when you least expect it. I've lived my life in the thick of danger. I've learned to grab what I want and not let go." His voice lowered. "That's you, Angie."

She claimed his mouth and ran her hands down his back, around and up his chest. Pleasure beaded along her skin as he severed the kiss and trailed a path down her neck. She licked and kissed her way down his chest, pausing to suck and nip his nipple. A groan escaped him as he reached for her.

Amusement rolled from her when he hauled her back

up and pinned her to the bed. Arms above her head, she smiled up at him. "Not fair. I want play time, too."

"Next time."

Angie writhed against Twitch's weight pressed against her. Legs wound around his lean hips, she savored the glide of his hardened cock against her wet pussy. "John, please."

"I love hearing you moan my name," he growled against her skin. He sucked her nipple. Heat spiraled from the aching bud and pooled between her legs.

She loved how he was never in a rush, as though he cherished every moment they spent together. Every day was a gift. She'd learned that the past several months while on the run. Urgency heightened her awareness as pleasure rolled through her.

"I can't wait any longer to feel you around me, Angel."

"Then don't," Angie panted.

A gasp escaped her as he powered into her in one deep thrust. Their mouths collided in a frenzied kiss. She dug her nails into his ass and matched his harried tempo.

"Home," he whispered in her ear. "Being inside you feels like coming home."

"John." She ran her hands up along his back and tightened her legs around him. Her breaths became labored.

"Come for me, Angie." He shifted her legs, raising them up so his thrusts into her went deeper.

She clung to him as her entire body tumbled into a euphoric bliss. She cried out in pleasure as she climaxed. John shouted his own release moments later.

Sated, she wrapped her arms around him and interwove their legs. She remained beneath him, relishing his weight as she drifted within the sensuous haze. "That was amazing."

"It's never been like that with anyone else," Twitch whispered. He settled her against him as he repositioned himself on the bed.

Angie rested her head against his chest and let her mind wander to what he'd said earlier. Ethan's offer might very well be the answer she'd been seeking. But what about her dojo?

"I'm worried about the dojo. What if everyone hates me now because of what happened? A murderer was teaching classes there. A psychopath was in those classes. What if I can't recover from all that?"

"You will," Twitch said. "From what I've seen, there's no way anyone in this neighborhood will blame you for shit you had no control over."

Angie hoped he was right. If they couldn't see beyond what'd happened and business at the dojo flagged, she'd always have Ethan's offer… one she was extremely tempted to accept if she could figure out how to make it work. She and Twitch would figure it out.

CHAPTER 18

Two weeks later...

Angie waited until the straggling teenagers left the dojo before she turned to her father. He'd taken over the class halfway through and had done very well. His unique militant-style leadership was, in many ways, exactly what a lot of the kids who took her class needed.

"You did well with them," she said.

"They're good kids." He wiped his face off with a towel, then grabbed his bottled water. "I've gotta admit it's been great getting workout time in. The last few years in INSCOM have had me too sedentary. Old farts like me aren't sent out as much as I like."

Angie took a deep breath and forged into the conversation path her dad had just created. The past week had been an adjustment in many ways. Twitch and the rest of the Counterstrike and Arsenal personnel had left eight days ago. Life had returned to normal.

The neighborhood reaction to Claude's arrest wasn't the huge fallout she'd initially worried about. Their shock hadn't translated to a mistrust in her or the dojo. The opposite happened, in fact. They'd come around more often. People she'd never met before introduced themselves and joined the dojo.

Media coverage of what'd happened had drawn in other martial arts experts, three of whom she'd offered part-time positions so she could vet them as potential instructors. In short, life post-nightmare was better than it had ever been.

The FBI and Philadelphia police department moved swiftly on pressing charges against Chastity and Claude, as well as her father. They'd also released Eric and cleared him of all charges. Thanks to Claude's cooperation in exchange for federal protection, none of the crime family would see the light of day anytime soon.

Angie regretted that she hadn't had a chance to speak with Claude again. He'd been enrolled in the witness protection program quickly, and from what she'd heard, he'd be cleared of most charges because of his testimony. Although he'd made some rotten decisions and had clearly done some terrible things, she hoped he had a happy life. He deserved the fresh start he'd hoped to find at the dojo.

Agent Blevins had even figured out why Noah Wints had inserted himself into Angie's world. Ethan had been right—he was nothing more than an idiotic and horny playboy who'd thought she'd be an interesting lay.

She and Twitch chatted daily, often three or four times. Every night ended with a long, very enjoyable video chat. While she couldn't wait to see him in person, their long-distance relationship was progressing well.

"You're thinking pretty hard right now, Angel Eyes." Concern flashed in her father's gaze as he sat on a bench. "Things okay with Twitch?"

Twitch. Her heart warmed every time she heard her father use the nickname. Approval filled his face whenever he spoke about Twitch or Counterstrike or The Arsenal.

"Things are great. I've been meaning to talk to you about something, though. Ethan has an idea, a very good one."

"Doesn't surprise me. Those two boys have one hell of an organization. There's nothing Ethan and Milo can't do when they put their minds to it." He rested his back against the wall. "What can I do to help? Read me in."

Angie smirked. "They want dojos and youth centers across the country in every major city. Safe havens for people who need help. There'd be operatives there to handle protective and investigative services, all pro bono."

"That's one hell of an idea. I'm assuming it'll be tied to whatever it is The Arsenal's running."

Angie tightened when her father's gaze narrowed.

"This is a talk between you and me, Angel Eyes. I've heard enough scuttlebutt to know there's one hell of an underground operation running to help people in trouble. I know The Arsenal's behind it and Counterstrike is involved." He reached out and took her hand. "I'm all in to do whatever I can to help. What they did for you..."

Tears filled his eyes. He blinked them away.

Her eyes burned as she forged ahead. "Ethan wants me to help. Twitch and I would be in charge of establishing the youth centers and dojos. He'd handle the business and operative side while I vetted and trained instructors and got classes going."

"You and Twitch, huh." Amusement flickered on his face. "He's one hell of a guy."

"He is."

"It's a good idea, but you've put a lot of work into this place. What'd happen to it?" Her dad looked around. "Those kids rely on you. So do the women and others who come in. What you're doing here is important."

"It is." She squeezed her dad's hand. "It'd be the first established waypoint for the new brick and mortar network. I'm trusting you with this, Dad. No one can ever find out the truth. There is a network, a huge and very complex one that's run by The Arsenal. It's an amazing thing, Dad. It saved my life."

Tears shimmered in her gaze. "I want to help give that to others. I need to pay it forward. This dojo would be a place anyone with trouble could walk into and get the help they needed, no matter what it is."

"Then do it, Angel Eyes." He wiped a tear from her face. "Your mom would be so proud of what you're doing."

Her heart pounded harder. "I want you to take over here, Dad. Manage this dojo so I can help Counterstrike create more like it."

The man's gaze swept the large room. "I'd love to. It'll take me a while to get the retirement pushed through. I'm close enough to the date to make it happen early."

"You don't have to do that. We can make it work until you're officially retired. We'd have whatever staff you needed here."

"What'd you say about operatives?"

"The Arsenal has operatives that aren't on mission teams. Once they've completed their training, they'd be assigned to a network operations team. There'd be a team leader, and they'd be moved into the area."

"They'd be here at the dojo? That'd draw a lot of attention."

"That part is still fluid. We'd test what works and doesn't work here." She looked around. "We'd test everything about this concept here. And in San Antonio once it's open. This would be the dojo portion. San Antonio would be the youth center."

"Sounds like someone's put a lot of thought into this already."

"Twitch and I sketched out some things."

"It's all a great idea, but I see a lot of problems. A team of Arsenal-trained operatives in every city is a lot of overhead. That'll make the cost of this help people can get too steep for most folks."

"No one would pay." Angie lowered her voice to a whisper. "I can't say much about this until you're retired and officially involved in this, Dad, but The Arsenal has the cost covered. What they don't have covered, Ethan and Milo do through Counterstrike. But, when Ethan pitched this to The Arsenal, they agreed on the condition they handle the overhead expenses for the teams and investigative and protective details. Counterstrike covers the overhead for the dojos and youth centers."

"The Arsenal has it covered." Her dad chuckled. "One of these days we'll sit down and I'll tell you about those two women they've got over there. Quillery and Edge. I should've known they'd have things sorted. Not much gets past them, and I'm seeing that not much gets past your man either."

"We're starting off small. San Antonio and here only until we work out all the kinks."

"I'm in." He looked into her eyes. "I'm proud of you, Angie."

"I love you, Dad."

"I love you too." He stood. "I'm thinking those two boys over there are getting a bit antsy. We'd best see what they want."

Angie looked up and smiled when she saw Benny and Clay standing there. She closed the distance and drew them both into hugs. "I was starting to think you were avoiding me."

"Nah. We had some shit we had to do," Benny said. His voice lowered as he looked at his brother. "We got bounced to another foster family."

Shit. Angie's stomach tightened. "You good?"

"We're better there than the other place," Clay said.

"Love the murals you've done," Angie said with a smile, opting to steer the conversation away from their troubles. There'd be time to discuss their living situations later. "I heard you have a couple more business booked."

"Yeah. And they're paying gigs," Benny said with a smile. "Wouldn't have gotten those without you."

"Tell her about the other shit."

"Nah. It ain't for sure," Benny said. He shuffled his feet and looked down. Then his gaze locked on to hers. "Someone saw what we painted here. He thinks I've got talent and wants me to do it on canvas. Says he can sell it in a studio."

Unease pricked Angie's skin. While the offer sounded great, she never trusted offers strangers made to kids. "Do we know this person?"

"Nah. He just walked up to me on the street. Said I had talent."

"Some rich dude who has friends with a gallery," Benny's brother said. "Can't remember his first name 'cause it was weird. Last name was Davenport, right, Benny?"

Angie chuckled. "Milo Davenport?"

"Yeah. That's him." Benny's eyes widened. "You know him?"

"Yeah, I know him. He's a good guy. You should follow-up, see what he thinks."

Angie couldn't believe how much her world had changed because of Twitch and Counterstrike. She looked forward to the work she'd do alongside them.

* * *

One week later...

"I love you," Angie whispered. Her beautiful hair tumbled across the pillow as she peered at him.

Twitch reached out and stroked her image on the monitor. Spending time via video conferencing every night was a sad replacement for the real thing, but better than nothing. If he closed his eyes, he could almost feel her touch, taste her sweetness on his tongue.

Long distance relationships sucked. He'd flown to

Philly twice since leaving Angie. Both times had been too brief.

"Love you too," Twitch said as a knock sounded at his door. "I'd better get going. Bea and Ryan are here. It's game day."

"Give him a big hug for me. He's gonna kick butt just like his uncle does." Angie grinned. "Later."

Twitch clicked off the video feed and shut his laptop. He headed for the front door and opened it. Bea, Ryan, Hazard, and his mom entered. The knee replacement surgery went well and his mom's recovery had gone much better than expected—mainly because Ethan had hired a private physical trainer to work with her.

"Oh, dear. Did we come by too early? We heard you chatting with Angie. You shouldn't have ended the call. We would've waited," his mom said, a twinkle in her gaze as she leaned on her walker. That twinkle was always around whenever she mentioned Angie.

"We'll chat again later tonight. She had to get to the dojo for a class soon anyway."

"I heard her dad's retiring a few months earlier and taking over the dojo," Hazard said. Amusement glinted in his gaze as he raised his eyebrows and in a not-so-subtle conversational shove.

Twitch had put off this discussion long enough. He ran his hands through his hair as Ryan hopped around the living room, his game day energy already at a high. He kicked Hazard's leg and did a loud shout. The man feigned an injury and fell to his knees.

Twitch laughed as the two began rough housing on the

ground. Bea sat in a chair and watched, her expression confused. Haunted.

"Been meaning to chat with you all about something," Twitch said. "My position at Counterstrike has changed."

"Oh?" His mom sat on the sofa. Twitch moved the walker to sit beside the end table nearest her. "A promotion?"

"Kind of." Twitch sighed and glanced at Hazard, who'd shuffled Ryan and himself to a seated position. Both peered up at him. "We're opening youth centers and dojos across the country. They'll offer the same services Angie does at hers in Philly and what we'll be doing in San Antonio."

"They'd be safe havens for people who need help," Hazard said.

Twitch let the man explain what they'd be doing at the dojos and youth centers. He sat beside his sister and took her hand when the conversation died.

"I'll be in charge of the new facilities," Twitch said. "That means I'll be in Austin less."

Bea's gaze lighted to Hazard, then returned to him. "You think I can't handle that."

"You've changed the past few weeks, sis. In a good way. You, Ryan, and Mom are the most important people in my life, but Angie's part of that now too. We'll be working together to open dojos and centers around the country. I need to know you all will be okay without me around as much."

Bea nodded. "I've learned a lot the past few weeks. I see now I haven't been in a good headspace since..."

Since leaving her abusive ex.

"I've started seeing someone, a counselor," Bea whispered. "Ryan has, too."

Shock rolled through Twitch. He hadn't known.

"I'm ready, John," Bea whispered. "We all are. Having you and Ethan and Milo and everyone else helping out, getting us through..."

Her voice broke as tears shimmered in her eyes. Twitch cursed and drew her into his arms. "I love you, Bea. There's nothing I wouldn't do for you."

"I know. I've always known. But it's time I sort things out on my own. I can't live life scared it'll happen again."

"It'll never happen again," Twitch growled.

"I'm starting to see that now," Bea whispered. "I saw that because of Angie."

Twitch tightened.

"She's an amazing woman," his mom added.

"She's perfect for you," Bea said. "Seeing her get through what happened to her, I see now I've been scared to live my life. I owe it to Ryan and to myself to be stronger, stand on my own."

"You aren't ever alone," Twitch said.

"I know." Bea squeezed the arm around him tighter. "But I'm saying we'll be okay. We all will be."

A knock sounded on his door. Startled, he stood. "Was Ethan coming over to go with us?"

"Dunno." Hazard said, amusement in his voice. "Answer it and find out."

Twitch opened the door and froze. Angie powered into him. He took a step back with the impact as she wound her arms and legs around him. Her lips locked against his. A moan sounded from him as he deepened the kiss.

Pleasure surged through him and hardened his dick.

"Wow. They're really happy to see each other! Uncle Milo says those kind of kisses are what makes babies. Uncle Ethan and Aunt Mari kiss like that all the time." Ryan's raised voice echoed within the room.

Angie severed the kiss. Laughter tumbled from her. "Surprise."

The whispered word in his ear warmed his insides. "Fuck, it's good to have you in my arms. You little minx, you weren't in Philly, were you?"

"Nope. I got in late, late last night and crashed at Ethan's and Milo's."

A rumble rolled from Twitch. Then his gaze settled on the open door and the baggage piled up outside. He stifled the irritation that she'd stayed anywhere but his place last night.

"Dad's out and taking over Monday morning," Angie whispered. "Ethan said I could use the jet whenever I needed to fly up for a day or two and help out at the dojo. Otherwise, I'm based here in Austin. Or wherever you'll be."

She kissed his throat. He tightened his grip on her waist as he processed what she was saying.

"Assuming you don't mind me moving in with you."

Mind? He was fucking thrilled—so much so he wished to hell his nephew didn't have a game. He'd love nothing more than to carry Angie to his bed and make love to her the entire weekend.

"Fuck, I love you," he declared loudly.

Loud sighs came from his mother and sister. Ryan laughed. Hazard chuckled and slapped him on the back.

"She wanted to surprise you," the man said. "Hate to say it, but the celebration will have to wait. We've got a game to get to."

"I love you, John," Angie whispered. "I can't wait to start our life together."

ABOUT THE AUTHOR

Born in small-town Texas, Cara Carnes was a princess, a pirate, fashion model, actress, rock star and Jon Bon Jovi's wife all before the age of 13.

In reality, her fascination for enthralling worlds took seed somewhere amidst a somewhat dull day job and a wonderful life filled with family and friends. When she's not cemented to her chair, Cara loves travelling, photography and reading.

Newsletter|Facebook|Twitter

OTHER BOOKS BY CARA CARNES

The Arsenal Series

Jagged Edge

Sight Lines

Blood Vows

Zero Trace

Battle Scars

Impact Zone

Counterstrike Series

Protecting Mari

Justice for Angie

There are many more books in this fan fiction world than listed here, for an up-to-date list go to www.AcesPress.com

You can also visit our Amazon page at: http://www.amazon.com/author/operationalpha

Special Forces: Operation Alpha World

Christie Adams: Charity's Heart
Denise Agnew: Dangerous to Hold
Shauna Allen: Awakening Aubrey
Brynne Asher: Blackburn
Linzi Baxter: Unlocking Dreams
Jennifer Becker: Hiding Catherine
Alice Bello: Shadowing Milly
Heather Blair: Rescue Me
Anna Blakely: Rescuing Gracelynn
Amy Briggs: Saving Sarah
Julia Bright: Saving Lorelei
Victoria Bright: Surviving Savage
Cara Carnes: Protecting Mari
Kendra Mei Chailyn: Beast
Melissa Kay Clarke: Rescuing Annabeth
Samantha A. Cole: Handling Haven
Sue Coletta: Hacked
Melissa Combs: Gallant
Anne Conley: Redemption for Misty
KaLyn Cooper: Rescuing Melina
Liz Crowe: Marking Mariah
Sarah Curtis: Securing the Odds

Jordan Dane: Redemption for Avery
Tarina Deaton: Found in the Lost
Aspen Drake, Intense
KL Donn: Unraveling Love
Riley Edwards: Protecting Olivia
PJ Fiala: Defending Sophie
Nicole Flockton: Protecting Maria
Michele Gwynn: Rescuing Emma
Casey Hagen: Shielding Nebraska
Desiree Holt: Protecting Maddie
Kathy Ivan: Saving Sarah
Kris Jacen, Be With Me
Jesse Jacobson: Protecting Honor
Silver James: Rescue Moon
Becca Jameson: Saving Sofia
Kate Kinsley: Protecting Ava
Heather Long: Securing Arizona
Gennita Low: No Protection
Kirsten Lynn: Joining Forces for Jesse
Margaret Madigan: Bang for the Buck
Kimberly McGath: The Predecessor
Rachel McNeely: The SEAL's Surprise Baby
KD Michaels: Saving Laura
Lynn Michaels, Rescuing Kyle
Wren Michaels: The Fox & The Hound
Kat Mizera: Protecting Bobbi
Keira Montclair, Wolf and the Wild Scots
Mary B Moore: Force Protection
LeTeisha Newton: Protecting Butterfly
Angela Nicole: Protecting the Donna
MJ Nightingale: Protecting Beauty

Sarah O'Rourke: Saving Liberty
Victoria Paige: Reclaiming Izabel
Anne L. Parks: Mason
Debra Parmley: Protecting Pippa
Lainey Reese: Protecting New York
TL Reeve and Michele Ryan: Extracting Mateo
Elena M. Reyes: Keeping Ava
Angela Rush: Charlotte
Rose Smith: Saving Satin
Jenika Snow: Protecting Lily
Lynne St. James: SEAL's Spitfire
Dee Stewart: Conner
Harley Stone: Rescuing Mercy
Jen Talty: Burning Desire
Reina Torres, Rescuing Hi'ilani
Megan Vernon: Protecting Us

Police and Fire: Operation Alpha World

Freya Barker: Burning for Autumn
Julia Bright, Justice for Amber
KaLyn Cooper: Justice for Gwen
Aspen Drake: Sheltering Emma
Deanndra Hall: Shelter for Sharla
Barb Han: Kace
EM Hayes: Gambling for Ashleigh
CM Steele: Guarding Hope
Reina Torres: Justice for Sloane
Stacey Wilk: Stage Fright

Tarpley VFD Series

Silver James, Fighting for Elena

Deanndra Hall, Fighting for Carly
Haven Rose, Fighting for Calliope
MJ Nightingale, Fighting for Jemma
TL Reeve, Fighting for Brittney
Nicole Flockton, Fighting for Nadia

As you know, this book included at least one character from Susan Stoker's books. To check out more, see below.

SEAL of Protection: Legacy Series

Securing Caite

Securing Brenae (novella)

Securing Sidney

Securing Piper

Securing Zoey

Securing Avery (May 2020)

Securing Kalee (Sept 2020)

Delta Team Two Series

Shielding Gillian (Apr 2020)

Shielding Kinley (Aug 2020)

Shielding Aspen (Oct 2020)

Shielding Riley (Jan 2021)

Shielding Devyn (TBA)

Shielding Ember (TBA)

Shielding Sierra (TBA)

Delta Force Heroes Series

Rescuing Rayne (FREE!)

Rescuing Aimee (novella)

Rescuing Emily

Rescuing Harley

Marrying Emily (novella)

Rescuing Kassie

Rescuing Bryn

Rescuing Casey

Rescuing Sadie (novella)
Rescuing Wendy
Rescuing Mary
Rescuing Macie (Novella)

Badge of Honor: Texas Heroes Series

Justice for Mackenzie (FREE!)
Justice for Mickie
Justice for Corrie
Justice for Laine (novella)
Shelter for Elizabeth
Justice for Boone
Shelter for Adeline
Shelter for Sophie
Justice for Erin
Justice for Milena
Shelter for Blythe
Justice for Hope
Shelter for Quinn
Shelter for Koren
Shelter for Penelope

SEAL of Protection Series

Protecting Caroline (FREE!)
Protecting Alabama
Protecting Fiona
Marrying Caroline (novella)
Protecting Summer
Protecting Cheyenne
Protecting Jessyka
Protecting Julie (novella)

Protecting Melody
Protecting the Future
Protecting Kiera (novella)
Protecting Alabama's Kids (novella)
Protecting Dakota

New York Times, USA Today and *Wall Street Journal* Bestselling Author Susan Stoker has a heart as big as the state of Tennessee where she lives, but this all American girl has also spent the last fourteen years living in Missouri, California, Colorado, Indiana, and Texas. She's married to a retired Army man who now gets to follow *her* around the country.

www.stokeraces.com
www.AcesPress.com
susan@stokeraces.com

Made in the USA
Monee, IL
02 June 2020

32413170R00154